Running AWAY

Book 4 of The Ravaged Land Series.

By
Kellee L. Greene

This is a work of fiction. Names, characters, organizations, places, events and incidents are either products of the author's imagination or are used fictitiously. Any resemblance to actual persons, living or dead, events or locales is entirely coincidental.

First Edition September 2016

Chapter one.

I would never feel safe again. Not in the way I once had… before my life had been turned upside-down. It wouldn't matter where I was or who I was with, there would always be danger lurking around every corner.

Each and every mile we put between us, the resistance camp and the HOME army, help me feel a teeny bit better. But not much.

It was like I didn't recognize myself anymore. Even when I caught my reflection in the side mirror I didn't know who that girl was looking back at me. I wondered if the others felt the same.

This world had changed me, and I wondered if they had felt the same changes within themselves. It felt strange how we were all so close, yet at times I felt as though we were miles apart. Stuck deep within our own thoughts, struggling to make sense of this world.

Maybe we felt so far away from each other because we were trying to make ourselves forget about all the bad things that had happened. I knew I wanted to forget. In fact, forgetting was the only way to move forward.

Of the two resistance camps I was aware of, both were destroyed, but that didn't mean a whole hell of a lot. I knew there were more of them out there. But what I didn't know was exactly how many of them were scattered around or where they were. They could be anywhere.

The same was true for HOME. They had their main base in Alaska, of course, and maybe other large bases, and they also had their army camps spread all over. Not to mention the spies they employed to wander around looking for recruits.

HOME had invaded the resistance camp we were in and took out everyone and everything that was inside. I was positive they would make sure to eliminate anything they deemed a threat to them and their cause. They would obliterate those that were against them, until they were the ultimate power.

"You OK?" Penn asked keeping his eyes focused on the road.

"Mmm hmm," I said with a small nod. I pulled at my seatbelt as if I was suddenly uncomfortable.

"Seems like you are on another planet," he said letting the corners of his mouth curl upwards.

"Ha! I wish," I said looking up at the sky. Was it better out there? It had to be.

I stared at the sky thinking that we'd been lucky so far. Sort of. We had narrowly escaped HOME's clutches, and only because I had done something I wished I wouldn't have to carry with me the rest of my life. Something I wouldn't ever truly forget, but for now, I'd shove it deep down inside me like I sometimes had to do. I tried not to think about it, and it was something I hoped I'd never have to talk about again.

4

What I had done to Ryan was hidden away right next to everything else I had seen or done that I wished I wouldn't have. It was locked up in a closet surrounded by all the good memories that would warm my heart. Those thoughts kept me going. Love. Dreams. Fun.

If it hadn't been for Penn's quick thinking, we would have been without our guns after the confrontation with Ryan. I dropped mine after pulling the trigger and Dean had lost his. But at some point, Penn had given me my gun back, and he gave one to Dean as well.

I was pretty sure the gun he gave to Dean wasn't the same one he originally had, but I guess in the end that doesn't really matter. The few times I'd see him pull it out, I looked at it wondering if it had been Ryan's. But mostly I forced the thought away. It was just a gun. And having a gun was more important that not having one.

As we drove down the lonely highway, I couldn't help but imagine each turn we took would take us to one of the HOME camps or one of the resistance camps. We knew there were more of them but since we didn't know where they were it felt like it would be impossible to avoid them. But I guess on the bright side, at least we were aware of their existence. We could be cautious.

Penn had even speculated at one point that he believed there were other HOME bases out there, like the one that they had in Alaska. Similar to the one I had spent some time inside of. There could be even more of those huge campuses full of people falling in line with HOME's plans. Never questioning them or their motives… just happy to have somewhere safe to be.

Ever since we found the camp in Seattle, I couldn't help but wonder if they were out there constructing more and more of them. One day their bases would be like cities, strategically placed over the whole Earth. They would control the world.

Dominick had thought they had every intention of taking over the world and he had probably been right. It was the only thing I think I agreed with Dominick on. But Dominick wasn't alive anymore to spread his message. Maybe the rest of the resistance could get the word out, but for some reason I didn't think so. It wasn't like having the resistance in charge would have been any better. Things would never be how I would want them. The way they should be.

What we needed to do was continue to travel east until we could find somewhere we could call our home. Somewhere we could stay safe and hidden from all the camps and bases and crazy people trying to stake their claim and lead what was left of the Earth's population.

"Michigan," I said breaking the silence. I turned to look at Penn, but he didn't return the look. He narrowed his eyes at my words but kept his focus on the road ahead. I knew he had heard me but I couldn't tell what he was thinking.

I shifted my eyes back towards Dean who was rubbing his injured arm. The arm that had taken a bullet from Ryan's gun. He rubbed and poked it so much it was almost like he enjoyed feeling the sting of the pain. Maybe it reminded him he was still alive.

Dean had been only inches away from death when Ryan had that gun pointed at him. He would have done it too. It was a miracle that he missed and it only badly grazed Dean's arm.

"Maybe," Dean said shrugging his good shoulder.

"Why Michigan?" Sienna asked, leaning forward slightly taking an interest in the conversation.

"Seems like there should be a lot of water up that way, and maybe some farmland we could use too," I said not exactly sure why I picked Michigan. Mostly it felt like a random pick, but it would have water and fishing. It seemed like a good choice even though other states probably would have fit the bill as well. It also seemed like it may be secluded, or isolated from what was going on, but that was merely a guess.

Anyone that had survived this long was probably out there looking for others. Not running from them, as we were.

Further east I guessed there might be more camps and bases. Places that had larger populations were probably at the top of HOME's list for growing their numbers. At least that's what I imagined. Those were the places I wanted to avoid. As long as we could stay out of trouble along the way and got to northern Michigan, I figured we could be safe for a very long time. Well that was my hope anyway.

Somewhere completely isolated from the world before everything had happened would probably be best. Like somewhere up in the Canadian wilderness, or maybe even a deserted island. But Canada would be cold and snowy in winter and how would we even get to an island? Not that I even knew how to go about finding an island we could live on. Hawaii? The Bahamas? Cuba? Clearly my knowledge of islands was pretty limited.

Michigan would be cold and snowy in winter too, but it wouldn't be bad if we were ready for it. If we could stock up supplies and have wood for a fireplace. And if I was wrong, we could worry about the alternatives later.

"Are there any objections to Michigan?" Penn asked.

"Not a single one I can think of," Dean said smiling at me. I couldn't help but smile back. We had been through so much together and now, maybe, we'd finally be able to find somewhere we could just stop and take a break from all the horrible stuff. We could just be together.

"Fine with me," Sienna said, flashing me a bright smile. A smile that was so similar to Dean's even though nothing else about them was. The brother-sister love they had for one another was forever. He would take care of her no matter what and she would let him.

Sienna gripped my arm and started shaking it excitedly. Even without Penn's vote, it was decided. We were going to Michigan to find our home.

"All right, here we come Michigan," Penn said, keeping his face neutral. "Let's just hope there are no HOME bases or resistance camps there. If there are, I don't know what we'll do. How long will it be until HOME is everywhere?"

"No kidding. We can't get involved with either of them. HOME is probably still out there looking for us. And let's not forget how we met the resistance… they kidnapped us and practically forced us to join at gunpoint," Dean said squeezing his eyebrows together. The only good thing about the resistance was that they weren't searching for us. If we ran into them again, they likely wouldn't kill us on the spot.

"If I'm wrong about Michigan, then somewhere else… there has to be something. We'll figure it out," I said sounding somewhat optimistic.

I felt unusually comfortable. Maybe even too comfortable. We had tons of supplies packed in the back, a destination in mind… the only thing we had to worry about was finding gas along the way.

We had our cut-up hose for siphoning, but the cars we'd found so far had mostly already been emptied. Gas was a precious commodity. And all the empty tanks were an indication that it wasn't just us out here looking for gas along the roadways.

So far we'd managed to find enough, but I wondered how long it was going to last. Eventually the gas would run out for everyone, but the goal was to be in Michigan in our new home by the time that happened. Once we were there, we wouldn't need gas.

Sometimes I wondered if we left Utah too soon. We only stayed about a day before packing up the car and heading out east to get as far away as we could. The house we had been staying in was well stocked, but it was too close to the HOME army. Then again, everywhere felt too close to the HOME army.

I leaned back and allowed myself to daydream about how perfect life could be once we found our new home in Michigan. Of course, deep down I was also being realistic, but it helped the time go faster if I was imagining about how nice it was going to be.

We could build ourselves a fortress, and if anyone came wandering around... well, we'd still have our guns just in case. Maybe we could set up traps or something to keep ourselves safer. We could build a fence and line the top with barbed wire.

If we ever managed to get ourselves safe, I'd probably sleep for twenty-four hours straight. Maybe even longer. I had a lot of sleep to catch up on. We all did.

We could even try to build ourselves an underground shelter. If HOME ever decided to let their deadly storms loose again, we'd have somewhere we could hide from them. It probably wouldn't be anywhere near as safe and secure as Ryan's grandpa's shelter had been, but it would be better than nothing at all.

"Oh crap," I said when I noticed movement in the ditch up ahead of us. We were still far enough away that I couldn't tell exactly what was going on, and I was pretty sure they hadn't seen us either. At least not yet.

It was a small group of people and it didn't

seem as though they were getting along. The last thing any of us wanted to run into right now was more people. And these people didn't seem friendly.

"Slow down," Dean said pulling on the back of Penn's seat. Penn let off the accelerator and let the car quietly roll to a stop

We were still a good distance back, and the group hadn't seemed to notice us. Penn didn't have to say anything for me to know he didn't want to get involved, or be seen for that matter. None of us wanted that.

"What's going on?" Sienna asked, her voice barely above a whisper. She likely already knew none of us had any better idea what was happening than she did.

"Not sure," Penn said, squinting at them while his hand gripped the shifter. He was probably considering putting the car in reverse and finding an alternate route.

We had taken a map from a gas station miles and miles ago, so I was pretty sure we could find another way. But it was far easier and much faster to stay on the highways.

One of the biggest reasons we took the interstates and highways was because the path was always clear whereas back roads weren't always as easy to navigate. Not to leave out the fact that the quality of the roads was deteriorating… more bumps, dips and pot holes. That could all lead to more risks to the car, like flat tires. The back roads also provided fewer opportunities to stop and look for gas and supplies.

"Are they hurting them?" I said as I squeezed my eyelids closer together so I could focus on the group of people. The group seemed to be trying to pull two of them back into a patch of trees off to the side of the road.

The two that were getting pulled were putting up one hell of a fight not to go with them. I figured it was only a matter of time before someone pulled a gun and ordered the two of them to go peacefully... or took care of them both once and for all.

"It looks like they're disagreeing about something. Whatever it is, it's not our problem," Penn said shifting the car into reverse and putting his hands on the steering wheel. I could tell he was getting ready to do something, like drive away.

"Wait," I said putting my hand on top of his forearm. "What if they are in trouble? What if they need help?"

"Not. Our. Problem," Penn repeated the words slowly.

I watched the group, trying to figure out what was going on. It looked like two of the eight, a boy and a girl probably around our age, were trying to get away. They were arguing and I could tell by how wide the girl was opening her mouth that she was shouting at the group of men. The boy stood close to her in a protective stance. It looked as though the group was trying to get the two to go back with them.

"This isn't a kidnapping," I mumbled as I kept my eyes on the girl. Her face was so red from all her screaming it almost seemed like she was going to pop. A couple of the others backed away from her looking nervous. Maybe they thought all her screaming was going to draw unwanted attention. Like from other people or maybe from the dog-beasts.

She raised her hand up to one of them as if she was making sure he wouldn't speak, and then she shouted at him some more. His face tightened and his hand stretched out and smacked her hand down. He grabbed her by the shirt and pulled her towards him at the same time he jerked his hand back. The boy stepped forward, but it was too late, the man had swung his arm forward and struck her violently across the face.

The force was so hard that when he let go of her shirt she took several side steps and fell to the ground. He grimaced and pulled back as if he was going to hit her again, but his face softened slightly and he looked away from her.

"Penn," I said pulling on his arm, "we have to do something!" I worried that the men were going to kill them. They looked nervous and angry, and that seemed like a volatile combination.

The girl put her hands over her face and I knew she was hiding the fact that she was sobbing. Based on her reaction to everything I didn't think it was the first time she'd been hit by that man. She didn't seem at all shocked or surprised.

The boy that had been at her side stepped forward. He didn't seem to have a weapon or anything but he wanted to show the man he wasn't afraid. He was going to take whatever blow the man was going to deliver. Maybe he would even fight back.

"Are they part of the resistance?" Sienna asked, her voice near a whisper. It seemed as though she was afraid they could hear her talking, but we were so far from them they hadn't even noticed our car driving towards them. Or us sitting here watching everything play out. They had been distracted with their dispute, or whatever it was that was going on.

"They could be... kind of looks like it," Penn said looking behind to make sure the path was clear to back up and leave. "I don't think they are HOME, that's for sure."

"Because they aren't dressed like HOME?" Sienna asked, still keeping her voice quiet.

"No, not because of their clothing. HOME isn't always running around in uniforms," Penn said, blinking several times as if he was trying to erase a thought that had popped into his head. I was pretty sure I knew exactly what he was thinking about.

"Yeah... you didn't have a special uniform on when you found Ros's cabin in the middle of nowhere," Dean said, trying to keep his voice neutral, but I recognized the tinge of lingering resentment.

Penn's deceit had felt like a lifetime ago, but he had easily tricked me when he had still been working for HOME as a spy. He had been dressed in normal clothing and nothing at all made him stand out as being connected to HOME in any way. Well, other than the hidden tattoo.

"These guys could be spies?" I asked raising

an eyebrow. There was something unpolished about them that made me think they were not. Not to mention that a group of people hanging out together fighting on the side of the road just didn't seem very spy-like.

There was a time I hated Penn for what he had done to me… to us. But now I trusted him with my life. I hoped I wouldn't come to regret that choice because, as far as I was concerned, he earned it.

Maybe I couldn't ever trust him the same way I trusted Dean or Sienna, but I trusted him as much as humanly possible with everything that was going on. He had done so much for us and he had saved my life more than once. I had to think it wasn't all some sort of larger plan and if it was, well, hats off to him.

I winced when the older man hit the boy our age. It was almost as if I could feel the blow myself. The boy stood there, his fists clenched, while he held his entire body absolutely still. The anger in his eyes was noticeable even from our distance. But still he didn't fight back.

Just when I thought it might be over, the man that had just hit him pulled out his gun.

Chapter two.

The man took a step closer to the boy and directed the barrel of his gun inches from the boy's nose. If it phased the boy at all, I couldn't tell. He kept his body steady while the girl on the ground leaned forward on her knees looking as though she was crying and begging for the man to stop.

Two of the group members looked on uneasily. One of them rubbed their nose as if it was a sign to the other one to retreat. They started backing away as though they didn't want to see what would happen if the man shot the boy. I didn't blame them.

The old man shook the gun in the boy's face as he yelled something, lowered his head and then let the gun fall gently to his thigh. The man looked up at the boy and shook his head. It looked as though the man had started sobbing. He almost looked as though he was in pain.

"This is crazy," Penn said, his eyes darting from man to man. I could feel his anxiety radiating out of his body, but for some reason he stayed. Even though his desire to leave was strong, he stayed… waiting and watching.

After a few minutes the older man pointed the gun at the guys behind him. The ones that I had thought were on his side. Almost all at the same time the men turned away and started running.

They all disappeared from view through a patch of spruce trees.

Then the older man's mouth started to move as he spoke to the boy and girl. The boy took her arm and pulled her up off of the ground. He wrapped his arm around her and they started to hastily walk away from the man… in our direction.

"Oh shit," Penn said as he looked in the rear-view mirror again, making sure the coast was still clear. The car was still in reverse, but Penn kept his foot on the brake.

The two walked towards us and I couldn't tell exactly, but it looked as though the boy spotted us. He squinted in our direction. Seeing a car on the side of the road wasn't an unusual sight, so he must have seen people sitting inside.

It seemed as though he wasn't at all worried about us. For all he knew we could have been HOME, but he seemed to care more about getting away from the man than anything else.

They were a good twenty feet away from the older man when he turned his head in their direction and raised the gun. His expression was no longer one of pain and sadness, those emotions had been replaced by anger and maybe even hate.

"Oh, no!" Sienna said pointing a finger straight in the man's direction. "He's going to kill them!"

The boy glanced back to judge their distance and must have spotted the gun pointing at them. He ducked and pulled the girl's head down just as the man let out a pop from the gun. They kept moving closer and closer to us.

I grabbed my seat with both hands, "We have to—"

My sentence was cut short when Penn hit the steering wheel with his fist, pulled out his gun and shifted the car from reverse into drive. He drove wildly towards the boy and girl hoping it would throw the older man off his guard. Surely he wouldn't be expecting a car to just pull off of the side of the road and speed towards the boy and girl.

It must have worked because he closed one eye and stared at us as if he was trying to figure out who we were. Or maybe he was just trying to make sense of what was happening, but after a long pause he changed where his gun was aimed.

Penn was quicker than the man. His gun was already out the window and perfectly aimed. The loud pop echoed inside the car causing my ears to ring.

Penn shot again before the man had even been able to pull his trigger. This shot must have landed scarily close because the man took off into the spruce trees in the same direction his pals had left.

"You missed," I said, teasing him about his shot. Of course it had to be difficult to drive and shoot.

"No I didn't," Penn said raising an eyebrow. It seemed he was implying that he had only intended to scare the guy, not hit him. And considering the look on his face, maybe it was the truth.

He pulled the car up next to the boy and girl, gesturing for them to get in. Sienna opened her door and they squeezed in next to her.

I glanced at Dean, who was holding his sore arm upwards. It looked as though he was in a quite uncomfortable position trying to make sure everyone would fit and avoiding any unwanted pressure against his bad arm. As soon as we could afford to make a stop, I'd offer to switch places with him and he could sit in the front.

The two of them were silent except for their heavy breathing, as Penn zoomed past the area the man had escaped through the trees. As we left, the girl turned around. I thought she was going to be upset about what she had to leave behind, but instead I watched as she raised up her middle finger towards the spruce trees.

Once their breathing returned to normal and we were far enough away from the whole ordeal, I turned back to have a closer look at them. They were clinging to one another as if maybe they were afraid of us. As if they were only just now worried about what new situation they had gotten themselves into.

The girl covered her mouth and let out a soft muffled cough. Her face was dirty, but she was still incredibly adorable. Even though she had a cute, round, youthful-looking face, I didn't think she could be much younger than I was. Her hair was snarled up in the back as if she hadn't combed it with anything but her fingers since HOME launched their weather weapon.

The boy she was with looked a few years older. He had dark blonde hair, maybe a shade or two darker than it would have normally been, because it looked as though it hadn't been washed in some time. But what really stood out about him was his cold, steel blue eyes. He looked strong, and it was almost as if I could reach out and touch the shell that he had built up around himself. I knew without a doubt, the only one he let inside that shell was the girl he was with.

They didn't even bother to try to hide their fear from us. It was as if they were already expecting the worst. I wondered why they had even gotten into the car, but I guess when they heard the gunshots they picked the path that seemed the safest at the time. I would have probably done the same and not even noticed if I was getting in a car full of HOME members on their way to the nearest HOME base.

"Are you OK? What's your name? Who was that man?" I asked, bombarding them with questions as fast as I could think of them. I looked at the girl first but she refused to hold my gaze more than a second. I turned to the boy and cocked my head to the side, "He was going to shoot you both, you know that right?"

"Yeah, I saw that," the boy responded. He looked at each one of us carefully as he held onto his sister protectively. He was sizing us up.

"We aren't going to hurt you," I said with a half-smile. "Well, unless you do something to us first. Who are you?"

"I'm Carter and this is my sister Alice," he said, and Alice finally looked at me, able to hold my gaze. She stared until she was forced to look away to cough.

I nodded and waited for her to finish coughing. She seemed as though maybe she was sick with a cold or something... too bad we didn't have any cough drops in the trunk.

I wasn't sure but maybe we had something from the last house that could help. I made a mental note to check our supplies at the next stop. Maybe even some headache pills would help her if her symptoms were minor enough.

It wasn't like I was about to tell them about the supplies in the back, at least not yet. I didn't know them, which meant I didn't trust them. Telling them about our stash could potentially cause problems since everyone was desperate for supplies.

Sienna wore a friendly smile even though they seemed wary of her too. She was trying to do her best to make them both feel more comfortable. Especially Carter.

When her eyes settled on him it was almost as if I could hear her mental swoon. The sparkle in her eyes revealed that she thought he was hot.

She looked at me as if she could sense me digging around in her brain. I raised my eyebrow at her and she shook her head as if she was denying my unspoken comments, teasings and questions.

"I'm Ros," I said introducing myself, and then I pointed at the others, "Penn, Dean and that's Sienna."

Everyone politely said hi to one another, except for Penn who just grunted and kept his eyes on the road. Without asking I knew he was suspicious of them and probably on some level regretted saving them.

"Who was the man you were trying to get away from?" Sienna asked blinking several times at Carter. He squinted at her. It looked as though he thought she might have something wrong with her eye, but then he smiled at her once she stopped the fluttering.

His smile quickly faded though, once he started to speak, "That was our dad."

"Asshole," Alice mumbled as she crossed her arms vigorously and pressed them hard against her chest. "Wish he'd been shot."

"So why would your dad want to kill you?" I asked not bothering to beat around the bush. If there was any reason they shouldn't be in our car with us, I had the right to know. It was for our safety, although, to be totally honest, the only negative vibe I got from these two was that they were frightened. Alice seemed more scared than Carter, but both were caught up in something they weren't exactly sure how to handle. But what they didn't know was that we were the good guys.

"Alice didn't want to be there any more, so I told him that we were leaving," Carter said, looking towards Alice as if he was waiting for her approval. "He said we could leave, but he followed us out to the road. No one really gets to leave."

"Leave?" I asked wanting to know where they were and what place wasn't going to allow them to leave. I could have made two guesses, and one of them would probably have been right.

"I guess he probably thought we wouldn't actually do it. But we did. We were both done with that place."

"Leave where?" Penn asked, his voice clear. He didn't take his eyes off of the road, but I saw him take a sharp inward breath as if he was preparing himself to hear something that might force him to take action.

"His camp… the resistance. Are you in the resistance?" Carter said narrowing his eyes at me.

"No," I said quickly making sure there was no doubt about it. I didn't want him to think even for a second that any of us were part of the resistance. We were fully aware of the resistance and what those groups were capable of doing.

Alice started sobbing, "Oh God, Carter! It's worse! They're HOME! Dad was right! The only people left are HOME!"

"We aren't HOME," Penn said gripping the steering wheel so tightly his knuckles turned white. Alice instantly stopped crying with a sharp, short breath that almost sounded like a hiccup.

"Then who are you?" Carter said holding on to his sister even tighter. It almost looked as though he was ready and willing to jump out of the car pulling Alice out with him. "We don't want any kind of trouble. Just let us out and we'll be on our way. Thank you for everything you've done for us, but we'll be fine from here on out."

I watched under the headrest as he carefully moved his hand over to the door handle. If Penn stopped the car or slowed it enough, I was almost positive they'd make a run for it. What they didn't know was that we'd let them.

"We are just trying to find a safe place to go," Sienna said flashing her sweet smile at them.

She didn't want them to go. It was like she saw them as lost kitties and was wondering if we could keep them.

The problem was they were resistance. They couldn't be trusted. Even though they were trying to escape a resistance camp, which was definitely a point in their favor, it mostly sounded as though they were escaping their dad more than they were trying to escape the camp or its teachings.

"I don't understand," Carter said shaking his head. "If you aren't HOME and not part of the resistance, what group are you with?"

"We are just our own group, I guess. We are definitely not part of HOME or the resistance," I answered as I turned around in my seat to face the road. "It's just us."

Penn adjusted the rear-view mirror and I could tell he was doing it just so he could keep an eye on the two of them. He breathed heavily, "OK where can we drop you off?"

Chapter three.

"Penn!" Sienna said using a motherly tone. I curled my lips into a smile when I heard her click her tongue at him. If she would have had room in the backseat, she probably would have had her hands on her hips.

"No, don't worry about. It's alright," Carter said, his voice calm. I was tempted to turn around to see his expression, but it seemed as though he wasn't affected in the least by Penn's directness. "As far away as you are willing to take us."

Penn nodded and readjusted his mirror, as if that somehow made him feel better. It was as if he just wanted to know he could ditch them whenever he chose to. I wondered if it was because he didn't want to watch out for two people he didn't know or if he had other reasons.

"Where are you all going?" Alice said in a small but feisty voice. I could tell she could be a firecracker if she wanted to be. She was tough, but it didn't seem as though her shell was nearly at thick as Carter's was.

The only thing that really made me nervous about little Alice was her big cough. Every time that thick cough rumbled out of her chest I couldn't help but feel nervous. The last thing I wanted for any of us was to catch a cold on top of struggling to survive the already tumultuous conditions. Feeling under the weather wouldn't help someone be at the top of their game and completely aware of their surroundings, something that was practically essential.

"We're going to Michigan," Sienna said, her face morphing into an expression of worry. She looked back and forth between Penn and I as if maybe she thought she shouldn't have told them where we were going. I glanced at Penn but he didn't look away from the road. If it bothered him, he didn't let it show. "If you have nowhere to go —"

"Say," Penn said, barging into the conversation, "maybe you guys would like to go somewhere in Colorado. I'm sure you can probably keep your distance from your dad in the mountains."

I narrowed my eyes at Penn. The tone he was using was one I had heard before. It was similar to the one I had used when I tried to send him away when he stumbled upon my cabin in Alaska, starving to death. Now here he was, part of our group with no qualms about sending away people in need of a friend. And they probably weren't HOME spies like Penn had been. Apparently he didn't remember what it's like to receive help when you need it most.

"Sure, wherever you want to let us out," Carter said.

Alice coughed again, and I started to grow even more concerned. Not for her but for those of us around her.

I didn't know her in the least, but from what

I did know it didn't seem like she was about to pull a knife and kill me. If she had a knife, she probably would have pulled it on her father. They both seemed like fairly OK people from what little I knew about them. These were the type of people we needed to stick together with. Of course, they could be pulling an elaborate scheme and would take our stuff the second we let our guard down, but somehow I found that very unlikely.

"Why did you want to get away from your dad?" I asked trying to direct the question mainly towards Alice. I didn't look at her, thinking that if I was casual about it, I might get the most honest response.

"He's an asshole," she responded instantly.

"He is not a good man," Carter said, as if he was trying to erase her cuss word from the air.

Penn tilted the mirror again, and I was pretty sure he and Carter had connected eyes for a second. "Was that his camp?" Penn asked.

"Indeed," Carter responded.

I could only imagine what it would have been like for them at the camp. Could their dad have been worse than Dominick? I doubted it, but surely anything was possible.

"I'm done with him and that stupid camp," Alice said making a noise that sounded like she had slapped her knee. "I wish I could go with you guys… to Michigan. I've never been there."

"There isn't anything in Michigan," Dean said and it sounded as though he was taking Penn's side in the whole wanting to leave them behind thing. I was apprehensive, but I still thought they seemed normal enough and if they were truly good, normal people, we'd want them on our side.

They didn't seem to pose any real threat. More than anything else, they seemed as though they were just running away. Trying to get as far away from the crazy and all the danger... just the same as we were.

Alice coughed again. This time it was even more harsh than the others. It probably wouldn't be that difficult to find her cough drops or cold medicine. How many people out there were searching for those items? If we didn't have anything in the back, surely there was some still out there.

Penn glanced at me as if he was reading my mind. I could even have sworn I saw him shake his head at me. Only I didn't know if he was shaking his head because I was OK with them coming with us, or because I wanted to find her cold medicine.

"Then why are you going there?" Alice asked her voice hoarse and sharp like a razor blade.

"Because we are all done with this shi... what the hell?" I said looking out my window.

Dust was flying up into the air making a small brown cloud. At the front of the billowing dirt was a small fleet of dirt bikes and ATVs speeding towards us.

"Who are they?" Sienna asked looking out the side window.

"On this side too," Dean said tapping his finger against the window pane.

Penn glanced in the rear-view mirror, "And behind us too."

They were gaining on us at such a quick pace we'd unfortunately find out soon enough who they were. Penn sped up, but when another group appeared in front of us, he had no choice but to stop the car.

"Resistance?" Alice said and I could hear the fear in her voice. "Are these people with dad?"

"I don't know," Carter said in a hushed voice.

There was a line of cars, motorcycles, dirt bikes and ATVs blocking our path. Each one had a pathetic looking skull and crossbones painted on the side. A couple of the motorcycles even had flags sticking up in the air behind their seats, barely able to wave in the weak, nearly nonexistent breeze.

Penn looked as though he was going to start swearing but he punched the steering wheel instead. He probably blamed himself, think he should have been paying better attention. Maybe he even blamed Alice and Carter because he had been more concerned about what was going on in the backseat than our surroundings, but it wasn't his fault. I hadn't seen them descend upon us either.

One of the guys in their gang started pointing at Penn and laughing. Apparently he thought the angry reaction Penn was having was simply hilarious.

The men and women in the gang didn't look like they were from HOME. They looked rough and dirty, like they'd been out here struggling to survive, like the rest of us, for far too long. Although there were probably people from HOME that were out here struggling too, like Penn had been, but they probably weren't traveling the roads in a large group.

I tried to estimate how many of them were surrounding us, but it was hard to tell. Some of the men and women kept walking around, never taking their eyes off of our car. We were also constantly being circled by a few of the dirt bikes. My best guess was that there were maybe twenty-five or so.

They looked like a bunch of rejected prospects for a biker gang. The men and women all wore bandanas and some of the men had on leather chaps. The whole group was a spatter of brown dirt and black leather.

If they were armed, which they probably were, they kept their weapons concealed. And of course, so did we.

"Who's in charge," a man with an eyepatch said taking a half-step forward. He turned his head to the side but kept his good eye on us as he launched a big wad of spit towards the ground.

"Guess we should have appointed a leader… now what are we going to tell them?" I muttered, sliding myself down into my seat.

"I'll do it," Penn said, putting his hand on the door handle. Protesting wouldn't have done any good. He would have insisted he do it, probably mentioning the training he had that none of the rest of us did. Well, at least I assumed Carter and Alice didn't have any of the same skill-sets, but then again… maybe they did. If they were trained super-spies it would really help to know about it.

"Stay in your car," Patchy said, putting his hand behind him as he approached the car slowly with his other hand palm out towards us. "Put your hands where I can see them."

The way he spoke reminded me of how a police officer might handle a situation as he approached a questionable person. The way he moved and nodded towards one of his comrades was almost enough to confirm my thoughts. And if he had been police in a former life, he probably had fairly decent accuracy with that firearm he was no doubt hiding behind his back.

"Roll down your window... slowly," Patchy said looking into the window carefully as he sized us up. He shifted his eye back towards Penn, "No funny business now, you hear?"

"Right. No funny business," Penn said, but I knew that was only true if his group of pirates didn't do anything to piss Penn off. Although, we were drastically out-numbered. Penn also wouldn't do anything stupid.

He leaned down and looked inside the window, the same way a cop might. Patchy was extremely apprehensive. I wondered how many times he had done this same exact thing to other travelers. How many times had a traveler pulled a gun on him? Maybe that was how he had lost an eye. Or a knife to the eye? I didn't want to know.

"If you do as I say, this will go smoothly," Patchy said with his eye staring wide at Penn, and then he shifted it in my direction. I watched, waiting for him to blink, but he didn't.

"If I had a nickel for every time I heard that," I mumbled.

"What's that little lady?" Patchy asked even

though I was pretty sure he had heard me.

"Nothing, sir," I said in a way that one might respond to a police officer in the old days. I just wanted him to know I had him figured out. But if he got the message from my tone, he ignored it.

"Alright then, what you got in the back there?" he said speaking a bit slower. I noticed when he dragged out his words he had a bit of a Southern accent.

Penn turned his head and I could tell he didn't like where this was going. "*Our* stuff is back there."

"I'm sorry, but we're going to have to confiscate that stuff," Patchy said with a smirk.

"Of course you are," Penn said, as he looked over towards the surrounding men and women carefully. He was probably trying to figure out if there was any way for us to get out of here with our stuff... and our lives.

Patchy nodded to his men and four of them gathered at the back of our car. I pressed my hands against my face and slid them back into my hair. It was almost as if I was trying to wipe away my disbelief. We had been good on supplies, maybe we would have even had enough to make it all the way to Michigan, but now we would soon have nothing.

"Open the hatch," Patchy said knocking on the side of the car.

"Come... on!" Dean shouted hitting the back of Penn's seat with his palms. Patchy instantly reacted and raised his gun up cop-style. He pointed it at Dean as if he thought he was going to do something foolish.

Dean's hands flew up to show Patchy he was unarmed. Everyone in the area became very still as they watched Patchy. It was as if we were all posing for some kind of old-time hold-up photo.

Everyone was on edge. Some of the pirate-looking guys stared as they waited to see what Patchy was going to do. I wondered, in these situations, how often Patchy shot first and asked questions later. He probably didn't even bother to ask questions at all.

I briefly considered pulling my gun in case he was going to do something to Dean. They wouldn't at all be prepared for me to pull out a gun and start firing at Patchy. But, thankfully Patchy lowered his gun, so I didn't have to worry about turning into Calamity Jane.

"Open it," he said refusing to take his eye off of Dean.

Penn reached down to the keys hanging from the ignition and clicked the button that would pop the hatch open. He pressed his fingertips into his forehead and let out a big sigh.

"Yeah, sorry man. Times are bad for all of us you know," Patchy said, as if he felt guilty about taking our things. But if he did, that didn't stop him and his men from emptying the back of our car.

The guys walked past the car carrying all of our things. Not a single one of them looked at us. Patchy leaned over and looked into the car as he gestured at one of his people. A slender man carrying a hose and a gas can walked towards the car.

"Just one more thing… then you can be on

your way," Patchy said through the opened driver-side window. I looked at him, ready to swear at him, but when he wasn't wearing the sinister smile I expected, it threw me off guard.

Patchy walked away from the car before the slender man finished. The gang of road pirates stood there watching and waiting for the man to finish filling up their gas can.

The whole ordeal went by pretty fast. It seemed as though these road pirates had done this hundreds of times. We weren't their first victims.

The man walked away carrying the gas can and Patchy saluted goodbye to us as his group of pirates boarded their vehicles.

"Good luck," he shouted before he got onto his motorcycle. He started it up and the gang drove away leaving us stranded there on the interstate with nothing but the clothing on our backs.

Penn put his forehead down against the top of the steering wheel. There were a small handful of abandoned cars scattered around the highway, but I would have bet the clothes I was wearing that the road pirates had drained them a long time ago. We were going to have to set out on foot. At least we still had our guns.

Alice's cough broke the silence inside the car. I turned to look at her while her brother held her shoulders. The look on his face was a combination of concern and worry.

"How long has she been sick?" I asked looking at Carter.

"A couple weeks I think… it's a very stubborn cough," Carter said holding my gaze.

"Don't worry, I don't think she's contagious. I'm still fine and I've been with her every day since she came down with it."

I nodded. Of course that didn't mean I or the others couldn't catch whatever it was, but if Carter hadn't caught it yet, maybe we wouldn't either.

"Did any of the others in your camp get sick?" I asked narrowing my eyes at him.

"A few...," he said, as her coughing slowed. He turned to her, and she forced a smile indicating that she was done. "I guess this is where we should part ways."

Carter opened the door, swung his legs out and swiftly stood up outside of the car holding the door for Alice. Sienna looked at me and shook her head as if I should do something to stop them. It was painfully obvious she didn't want them to leave, but it wasn't up to me to beg them to stay. And I wasn't even sure if I wanted them to.

I looked to Penn to see if I could tell what he was thinking, but he still had his head down. Dean and I locked eyes, but he shrugged his good shoulder, probably having the same feelings I had.

Sienna folded her hands together as if she was begging for my approval. But I didn't know the right answer, and I couldn't answer for everyone. It seemed as though Dean didn't care one way or the other but without talking to Penn, I was pretty sure he didn't want them with us.

"Stay with us!" Sienna blurted out. Penn didn't raise his head but the groan he made sounded like he thought things just kept getting worse.

"Are you sure?" Carter said ducking down looking into the car towards Penn.

"No," Penn said not caring or bothering to hide his grumpiness. He sounded like a crabby old man that wanted the neighborhood kids off of his lawn. "We don't have any supplies, no car… you'll do better out there on your own."

"You have a gun," Carter said aiming his eyes at Penn's back. "We have nothing at all."

"For all you know we are lying and we're from HOME," Penn said turning to look at Carter. He lowered his head slightly so his eyes looked dark.

Carter shook his head, "You said you weren't."

"Oh. OK, well then. It's not like we could possibly lie about it," Penn said rolling his eyes. I wondered if he realized that he sounded like a big jerk. He must have, because he let out a big sigh. If I had to guess, he was probably just sick of all the bad things that kept happening to us. "I apologize for my behavior… if you'd like, you can come with us."

Sienna clapped her hands and rubbed Penn's shoulder. She slid out of the car after Alice and smiled at them both.

I got out of the car and surveyed the area. The orange ground was dry and dusty, and the air was warm. I looked both Carter and Alice up and down carefully now that we were closer. Even though I wanted to check them for tattoos, I resisted the urge. I was somewhat surprised, since they were resistance, that they didn't ask to check us over.

"So you'll come with us?" Sienna asked after Alice stifled a cough. Carter and Alice looked at one another and then at the exact same time they nodded.

"Let's go," Penn said, already at least ten feet from us. He was leading us away from the interstate. I moved my feet in his direction and hoped it wouldn't be a mistake leaving the road.

Chapter four.

I wasn't completely sure if we were even traveling in the direction we wanted to be heading, but Penn probably knew what he was doing. We had nothing. No water, and we were heading out into the Utah wilderness, but I knew he had his reasons for leading us this way. He didn't want to run into any more trouble.

We took frequent breaks… not because we wanted to, because we had to. We were all tired, hungry and thirsty. Penn repeated randomly that we weren't going to find water or food if we didn't keep moving.

"Are we even going the right way?" Sienna said trying not to sound like she was whining. But she was definitely whining. I was pretty sure even our new travel companions could tell.

"Yes," Penn shouted over his shoulder, barely glancing in her direction. He stayed a solid ten feet in front of us at all times. If I sped up to try to catch him, he just moved his feet faster. He was trying to scout out the area before the rest of us could get close. If there was danger lurking, he wanted to be the first to find it so he could take care of it.

Penn was probably looking for signs of HOME, the resistance, road pirates or other threats we weren't even aware existed. I had to hope none of those things would be out here in the middle of nowhere. Those people probably stayed closer to the roads where they could find supplies, if they needed them much easier than they would out here.

"Ah-ha!" Penn said showing his first smile since… well, I don't remember the last one. It was probably weeks ago, maybe months.

"What is it?" I said narrowing my eyes at him. He sounded excited which was definitely promising, but I was still worried. Nothing ever seemed to go our way… I didn't want to get my hopes up.

"It's water!" he said, kicking up some dust as he ran away towards the riverbank. I looked over my shoulder at Dean who was wearing a big, bright smile even though he was rubbing his wounded arm.

I picked up my pace and saw the beautiful river come into view. It was a fairly wide river with dark blue waters sparkling as it flowed gently.

The others surrounded Penn and me, and looked out at the river almost in disbelief. Penn was kneeling down on a rock, dipping his hand into the water as it rushed by. He lifted his hand up to eye level and turned it, letting the water run out, as if looking for something.

Alice ran up next to him and splashed her hands into the water. She formed a cup-shape and was about to suck down a mouthful of water when Penn swatted her hands down.

Carter took a step past me as if he was worried about what Penn might do. I stepped to the side blocking his way and looked up at him through squinted eyes.

"It's not safe to drink," I said, and Carter looked down at me as if I had been speaking another language.

"But what choice do we have?" Sienna said, shaking her head at me like I was the one stopping everyone from drinking the possibly bacteria ridden water.

It wasn't my fault. I wanted to drink it just as much as everyone else did, but we had nothing to filter or boil the water with. Not a single thing we could use to make the water safe to drink. Sienna was right, what choice did we have? We'd have to drink the water to stay alive.

"We should follow the river for a while... maybe there will be a house. We could find something to boil the water in," Penn said looking down at the river.

I looked around the area, and there wasn't a single house in sight. But if we found something, it would be worth it to make sure the water was safe to drink rather than getting sick from it.

It hadn't been that long since we'd last had water... maybe several hours since the road pirates took our stuff, but with all the walking we were very thirsty. I wasn't knocking at death's door, but flowing water looked very tempting.

"We might just have to risk it," I said feeling the dryness in my mouth. It had suddenly become all I could think about.

"Give it a little longer... just a few more miles and then if we don't find anything we'll risk it. Deal?" Penn said looking at each one of us. He even looked to Carter and Alice for their nods of agreement.

"All right," I answered last. It wasn't like I wanted to get sick from the water, or anyone else to for that matter, but no one was going to wait forever.

We walked along the river for at least two more miles, or so I guessed, but there wasn't anything in sight. No houses. No cabins. No random pots or bottles laying on the ground. Nothing.

"Penn," I said, stopping after Alice broke out into one of her coughing fits. I imagined a dry mouth probably wasn't helping with her cold. "I give up. Let's drink."

He lowered his head as if he knew better, and well I did too, but we were stranded. The water was moving so at least it wasn't stagnant. There hadn't been any animals around, at least that we'd seen, so hopefully it wouldn't be contaminated with animal waste. It looked clean, but I knew that didn't matter.

"I had to drink random water back when I was wandering around in Alaska," Penn said looking at the water as he spoke. "I never got sick from it."

And as if that was a green light, everyone moved up to the edge of the river and started scooping up water. I squatted down next to Dean and dipped my hand into the cool water. The small amount that actually made it into my mouth was almost instantly absorbed. I didn't even need to swallow. I quickly took another drink, and another… and then another.

We'd probably spent five minutes scooping water into our mouths. I wondered how much each drink increased our chances of ingesting something that could make us sick. But sick was better than dead so I drank and tried not to think about the microscopic yuckies that might be floating in each scoop.

"Let's keep moving," Penn said, gesturing as he jogged to get ahead of us. "We'll keep following the river."

None of us spoke as we walked along the lonely river. I focused on the sounds of the flowing water because when I listened to the water I didn't think. My mind couldn't go to the places where the bad and negative thoughts existed. All I heard was the water.

The further we walked, the stronger the water seemed to move. Penn kept glancing back to make sure we were all with him, at least that's what I guessed he was looking for.

There hadn't been any kind of shelter that we'd been able to stop at, or even somewhere we could stay for the night. Once day turned to night, I didn't know what we were going to do. It wasn't like I'd want to just sleep out in the open on the rocky, dirty riverbank.

"We shouldn't have left the road," Sienna said not even bothering to try to disguise her whining. She crossed her arms in front of her body. I couldn't tell if she was angry or just cold.

"You'd rather be in another resistance camp? Maybe with HOME? Or maybe dead?"

Penn said looking out over the river.

I couldn't be sure but it felt like we weren't heading in the same direction any more. The sun, when it randomly popped through the cloudy sky was no longer where it should have been.

If I had to guess, I think the river was pushing us southward which was the wrong way… we needed to be going east. Which seemed to indicate that we would need to get on the other side of the river.

"Of course not," she said matching his tone. I rolled my eyes and jogged to catch up with Penn. He was probably thinking the same thing about our directions when he didn't speed ahead.

I opened my mouth, but he stopped me, "I know… but I'm not sure what to do about it just yet."

"We can't afford to go too far out of our way," I said, but I knew he already knew that too.

He turned to look at me, but he didn't say anything. Penn ran his hands through his hair and turned to face the river again. "I think we are going to have to cross it," he said punctuating his sentence with a small grumble.

I glanced back at Dean who was squinting in our direction. He looked confused. Maybe he too had realized we were going the wrong way. Traveling on foot, in the wrong direction when we were already tired and without supplies was far from ideal.

"How do we do that?" I said knowing it was going to be difficult to get across the wide flowing river. The further along the river we walked the harder the water seemed to flow. If we had some rope we could have tied ourselves together, but we didn't have any rope.

"I'm not sure," he said as he stopped and turned to face everyone. "We are going to have to cross."

Sienna groaned and Alice's shoulders slumped down. She turned to her brother and shook her head as if pleading with him to come up with a better idea. But he put his hand on her shoulder and stared out at the river.

Dean stood next to me and took my hand. He bent down slightly and whispered, "I don't know about this, it could be deep."

"It's pushing us too far off course."

"Maybe we should come up with a new destination instead of trying to cross," Dean said, and I saw the worry in his eyes.

"We're in the middle of nowhere. What destination should we come up with?" I asked dropping his hand so I could cross my arms. It was as if I was shielding myself. And I was being a little stubborn, and I knew it. After all, I had been the one to pick Michigan, it kind of felt like a finish line. I could still see the perfect house in my mind and I wanted to get to it. It was waiting for me.

There wasn't anything out here for us. Even if we found a shelter, it would only be temporary until HOME or the resistance found us. They weren't that far away. Not to mention there wasn't any supplies out here and even if we found some the road pirates would probably just take it away again.

"OK, well… if you're both sure about it,"

Dean said but I could tell he wasn't completely on board. I was pretty sure he was just giving in because it was what I wanted.

Penn was looking out over the river as if he was trying to find the best path across. He walked five steps in one direction, looked around and then he went back the other way.

I walked over and joined him on a rock. I could sense his confidence was low compared to usual. Navigating a way across a river must not have been something they taught in HOME's super spy school.

"We'll cross here... locking arms," he said reaching out for my arm. I held it out and he twisted his arm slightly to link them. He gripped my forearm tightly and I grabbed his.

I copied the movement and locked my other arm with Dean's in the same way. He grabbed Sienna's arm, and she took Alice's. Carter gripped Alice's other arm and brought up the rear.

"Hold on as tight as you can," Penn instructed, although that seemed obvious. He took a deep breath and stepped into the water. "Oh shit!"

"What is it?" I said yanking him back towards the rock.

He pursed his lips and shook his head, "No... nothing, it's just cold."

I wanted to laugh but I couldn't. I was holding my breath as I was about to step into the brisk water.

The water came up to about mid-calf on my first step. Penn wasn't exaggerating, it was cold, but it didn't really hit me until I took my next step and the water was just above my knees.

"Ohhhh," I hummed as my teeth started to chatter. I wasn't thrilled with how quickly the water deepened. Looking out towards the river in front of us, I was sure that in three more steps the water would probably be waist deep.

Dean hadn't made any noise when he stepped into the water, but Sienna didn't bother to hide her little squeaky gasp. Alice either.

Fifteen steps or so later, I was about a third of the way across the river. The chilly water surrounded me and I felt as though if I couldn't use my arms, I might drown. We were going to have to let go of one another so we could swim.

Dean and Penn were both taller than I was so they didn't notice at the same time I did, but the bottom of the river was falling out from underneath me. Water splashed up against my face as I struggled to get my arms free.

When the water went into my mouth and nose, I started to panic. I coughed it out, but when I tried to tell them to let go, water filled my mouth.

Chapter five.

I instinctively started trying to get my arms free and Penn and Dean must have noticed because they let go. I dropped below the surface of the water flailing my arms and kicking my legs to get back up, but I wasn't coordinating my efforts because of the panic.

"Help!" I said in a gurgly voice as I popped above the surface. Penn grabbed onto my arm and raised me above the surface, holding me until I was able to calm down and regain control of my limbs.

Now that my arms were free I was fine. I could tread water to keep myself above the surface, although the current started to move me slightly.

"We'll have to swim across," Penn said as he swam back a little towards Sienna. She was managing to stay above the water, but she looked nervous. It seemed like she didn't want to take the last step where she knew she wouldn't be able to touch the bottom any longer. Penn looked her in the eyes, "It'll be OK. I'll help you."

Dean stayed close to me and I watched as Alice and Carter bravely and carefully lowered themselves into the deeper water. He watched her as they swam towards us.

Alice took two strokes before she started coughing. The cold water probably triggered it but it didn't stop her from swimming. Her already pale

47

skin looked white and her lips were blue, but she was determined and kept moving across the river.

I focused on the other side of the river as I swam with all of my remaining strength. The current seemed stronger in some parts of the river, which made it difficult. I was almost to the other side when I heard Sienna scream.

She wasn't there. Her head must have been below the water because I saw Penn furiously trying to reach down for her. When the look on his face changed, I knew something was wrong. He was swimming in circles looking around at the water.

"Sienna?" I screamed, but there was no answer. If she was underwater, she probably wouldn't have been able to hear me crying out for her.

Dean pointed at me and then at the other side before he turned to swim back out towards Penn. But the current picked up even more and practically threw him into me.

We were fighting against the current when I spotted Sienna's head pop up for a split second further downstream. I saw her gasp for air right before she was pulled back under.

"Go! Get to the other side," Penn shouted as he dove under the water towards Sienna.

Dean looked as if he didn't know what to do. I didn't have to ask to know that he felt as though he should go after his sister. But if he even tried, the water would probably push him under too, only making matters worse.

I looked upstream but I couldn't tell what

had caused the water to start moving faster. Whatever it was seemed to be worse right where Penn and Sienna were.

Alice and Carter were almost to the other side as Dean and I were still struggling to make it the last third of the way. I couldn't do anything but swim and let the water push me along, but once I was closer to the bank, I was able to stand and wade my way out of the river.

Once I felt I was safe, I turned to see if I could spot Penn and Sienna, but I couldn't find either. I walked along the riverbank scanning the surface of the water for either of them.

I couldn't even guess how far the current had pushed us downstream. It probably pushed Penn and Sienna even further, considering they were still in it.

Looking out at the water I could tell that it was raging even more the further downstream we walked. It was a white water rapid, and I worried that neither of them would make it out.

"Where are they?" I said unsure if anyone would hear me over the noise of the river rapids. I started to jog down the river, trying to be careful over the rocks and uneven terrain.

I barely noticed how much my body was shivering. The air was warmer than the water had been, but it didn't seem to matter. The water had chilled me to the bone. Or maybe it was because my friends were being pulled away from us by the raging waters and there wasn't a damn thing I could do about it.

"There!" Dean shouted and bolted past me

to the edge of a rock. I spotted Sienna's head bob up and down, and then back up again. Her arms were flailing around as if she was trying to tread water, but it was no use. There wasn't anything she could do to fight the rapids. They had total control over her body.

"Where's Penn?" I said scanning the surface for any sign of him. I felt my chest tighten when I couldn't find anything.

Dean shook his head as he grabbed my hand and pulled me along. Sienna was moving away from us so fast I was worried I'd lose sight of her. I just hoped she wouldn't get pulled back under. We had to do something, and fast, to get her out of the water.

When I saw Penn pop up about ten feet away from her, I almost felt relieved. But given the dangerous conditions there was nothing to be relieved about. They were both still in trouble and I could tell how true that was by the horrified looks on their faces.

Penn tried to swim along with the current in an attempt to speed up so he could catch Sienna. I worried he was moving too fast and would go right past her.

Every so often it would pull them down but they both seemed to fight their way back to the surface, or maybe they were just being jolted upwards by the raging torrent. It was impossible to tell.

Penn was about two feet away from Sienna when he lurched himself forward. He managed to grab onto her and she wrapped her arms around him, clinging to him like he was her life preserver.

We ran along the bank watching as they rode the rapids together. Penn was trying to steer them in certain directions but for the most part he was unsuccessful.

I saw a long, thick branch sticking out over the water and it appeared Penn noticed it too. He reached out for it but they were moving too fast. They jerked to a partial stop before the branch cracked and they were back to bobbing down the river. The branch floating along with them.

Penn lifted his hand up and I could see the deep shade of red washing down his wet hand. He'd cut himself on the rough bark from the tree branch. Penn grimaced and started scanning the side of the river for another branch.

We tried to keep up, but they were moving fast and it was difficult. My legs were so cold they felt stiff and the wet pants didn't help matters. It was hard to watch them and watch where I was stepping at the same time so I didn't break an ankle on the rough, jagged rocks that lined the riverside. I was pretty sure that if I sprained or broke my ankle out here, I'd be as good as dead.

They zipped downstream and their heads bobbed and disappeared frequently. It was hard to keep track of them. I watched as Penn lined himself up to attempt to grab onto another branch. This one looked bigger than the last. It curved out and almost looked like a giant arm reaching out to cradle them.

Their bodies hurled towards the branch and Penn didn't have to do much. Penn's body was thrust into the branch and it looked like he'd hit pretty hard. He quickly draped his arm over the big branch. They both looked like they were struggling to catch their breath.

"We're coming!" I shouted, but I doubted they could hear me over the loud noises of the crashing rapids. Penn was already pulling them along the branch towards the riverbank.

I was so happy they were going to be OK that I could barely hold myself together. They were both so important to me that I didn't think I could handle losing either of them, let alone both of them.

I had to stop and bend at the waist so I could steady my breathing and reign in my emotions. Watching them get washed away from us had been terrifying, although probably more so for them.

"You OK?" Carter said lightly placing his hand on my back.

"I'm fine... overwhelmed or something," I said through oddly spaced breaths.

I waved him away. If he stayed around worried about me I'd probably burst into tears. And for some reason I didn't want him to see me like that. Then again, I didn't really want anyone to see me like that, which is why I was doing my damnedest to hold myself together.

Dean reached out his hand to Sienna to help pull her to safety. I stumbled closer, trying to force my weak legs to work. I couldn't run to them even though I wanted to.

Once I hobbled my way to Sienna, I threw my arms heavily around her shaking, soaking wet body. "I'm so glad you're OK," I whispered into her ear and I could feel her head nod in agreement against my shoulder.

Carter and Dean were helping Penn out of the water and onto the rocky bank. Penn looked in our direction and smiled, but it wasn't a strong smile. It was forced. His arms and legs looked like they were made out of overcooked spaghetti noodles.

I couldn't smile back. I was worried about him. There was only so much a person could take. He was one of the toughest people I knew but it almost seemed as though things were getting to be too much, even for him. Penn's drive, strength and determination were being tested and I think he was aware of it. If he couldn't manage it, what chance did any of us have?

"Let's go," Penn said as he slowly made his way through our little group and back upstream. We probably had a mile or more that we had to cover to get back to the same spot we'd originally crossed the river. "We have to find a shelter."

"How's your hand?" I shouted towards him but he just waved it up in the air. I didn't see any major cuts or blood dripping down, so I figured he was fine. Although, maybe he intentionally showed me the wrong hand so I wouldn't pester him about something we couldn't do anything about.

I looked up towards the sky. We had a couple hours before the sun would start to fall and the world around us would be dark. Hopefully we could find something before then, but with how desolate things were around here, either from the storms or maybe it had always been this way, I didn't hold much hope for finding somewhere to stay.

Penn reached into his waistband and I knew he was checking for his gun. He gripped the handle tightly as if he wasn't really sure it was still there. I instinctively checked for mine and breathed a sigh of relief. At least if we had to stay outside for the night, we still had our weapons for protection.

But hopefully it wouldn't come to that.

* * *

We walked for several more miles before we decided to give up and find somewhere as secluded as we could. If we had to stay outside, we wanted to be as hidden as possible. The water would help because I was sure no one would be trying to cross it, especially at night. It would also give us something to drink, even though every time we drank the unfiltered water we were taking a risk. But we didn't have a choice.

We had our guns which would provide us protection, but that was all we had. And after everything we'd been through, all the swimming, walking and emotions, I was starving.

Everyone sat clustered together. Penn went back and forth about trying to start a fire. First, he would worry about having a fire and drawing attention and then he'd worry about not having one and freezing together in our wet clothes in the cold night air.

"It's going to get really cold," Carter said. I figured since he and Alice hadn't lived all that far away, they probably had a good idea of what it was like at night. It seemed as though he was gently urging Penn to make a fire without directly telling him to do so.

Penn looked up at the darkening sky. It wasn't dark yet, but it wouldn't be long before the sun completely disappeared below the horizon. I was pretty sure he had the knowledge to get a fire going if he needed to with whatever he could gather in the area. I could tell he wasn't sure what the right thing to do was.

"We have our guns," I said, sounding as though I was trying to persuade him, but I wasn't. At least not consciously. I wasn't sure what the right thing to do was either, but I wasn't excited about the idea of sitting out in the cold night in my still damp clothing without a fire.

Penn looked at me and then towards Sienna and Alice who were both sitting there trying to hide their chattering teeth and shivering bodies. If I wouldn't have been so focused on the feeling that my stomach was eating itself, my teeth probably would have been chattering too.

"OK, I'm going to make a fire," Penn said standing up and waiting for anyone to stop him. But no one did. He walked away from where we were sitting and started to scour the ground.

"I'll be back too," Carter said and quickly walked away before anyone could stop him to ask questions. I watched him as he put distance between us. I couldn't figure out what he was doing, but maybe he was just trying to find somewhere to go to the bathroom.

Penn came back with some dried pieces of thin grass-like stuff and rolled them loosely together. He dropped a couple pieces of wood down on the ground.

"I'm not sure I'm going to get this to work," he said without looking up. He had a long stick piece and another thicker strip of wood with a bit of a gouge in the side.

He placed the thicker piece down flat on the ground and the long one inside the little notch. His knee was pressing against the strip of wood holding it steady while he spun the stick between his palms.

After several minutes of twisting, a tendril of smoke came wafting out from the notch in the wood strip. Penn carefully placed the dried grass-like stuff on top of the small bit of smoking dust. He gently blew on the grasses until a flame magically appeared. Judging by the smile on his face, it looked as though he had even impressed himself.

Penn placed the sticks above the flame forming a teepee shape. Before we knew it, we had a warm, crackling fire.

"Where's Carter?" Penn said as he looked around at each of us.

"Right here," he said as he lowered himself down on one knee and carefully placed a big pile of leaves at his feet. "It's not much, but it's better than nothing at all."

"What is it?" Sienna asked squinting at the green leaves.

"Wild spinach," Alice answered, turning towards Sienna as if she couldn't believe she didn't know what it was. She shook her head and stretched out her palm.

I picked up a leaf and put it to my nose. It was something I'd had before… I recognized it as the same thing we had a few times back when we were in the resistance camp.

I popped the leaf into my mouth and chewed on it for far too long. It practically disintegrated in my mouth and I knew I'd need a lot more to fill up my empty stomach. But the pile of spinach he brought over wouldn't be nearly enough to fill any of us.

"Was there any more out there?" I asked looking in the direction he'd walked away.

"I'm sure there is," Carter said as he divided the leaves into perfectly equal piles.

"It's too dark," Penn said directing his gaze at me.

"Maybe we can try to find more in the morning," Carter said handing me one of the piles. "I'll show you where to find it."

Penn stared at him for a long moment, "You know a lot about foraging?"

"Only what I learned back at the camp from my dad," Carter said handing Penn a bunch of the leaves.

"What else did your dad teach you about?" Penn asked squinting at him, either because he was suspicious or because the fire was too bright. If Carter noticed, he didn't make anything of it. Maybe he expected to be scrutinized and questioned. And maybe he didn't have anything to hide.

Carter smiled and looked out towards the river. He popped a few of the leaves into his mouth and slowly chewed them before answering, "I know that if I had a long enough stick with a few carefully sharpened points at the end, I could probably catch us a fish."

Everyone in the camp stopped sucking on their leaves to stare at him. I wondered if they were all tasting fish as they ate their leaves. They were already seeing the fish cooking in the fire. Whatever. They could have their stinky fish and I'd stick to the leaves. For now.

"We can look in the morning," Penn said as he popped a leaf into his mouth. There was only a sliver of sunlight left. In only a blink it would be night. Our only light would be from the blazing fire Penn made.

Chapter six.

We took turns keeping watch throughout the night. At any given time though, there would often be more than one of us awake. It was difficult to sleep on the bumpy, rocky ground. Well, that and the fears about all the things that could go wrong.

From time to time Alice's coughing would wake up anyone that was asleep and then it would take them forever to fall back asleep. She'd mumble an apology, but sleep just wasn't easy no matter how badly we needed it.

When I saw the sun peeking up over the horizon I was glad night was over. And thankful that we hadn't been kidnapped or killed. We could finally stop trying to sleep and get on with our day.

Penn stood up and looked around the area as if it had somehow changed. He stood up to kick dirt on the fire when Carter raised up his hand to stop him.

"Wait… let me try to fish. It won't take long," he said as he walked away from us backwards watching to see if anyone would stop him.

When no one did, he turned around and practically skipped over to a tree. I watched him as he examined the random branches around the trees and those still on the tree. He reached up and easily broke off one of the branches with a big crack.

Carter wore a big smile as he made his way back over to the camp studying his branch. The long stick had three smaller branches that stuck out like pitchfork prongs. He crouched down next to a rock and started carefully sanding away at the wood. He was trying to sharpen the smaller branches that forked off into deadly little spears.

"It's safe to assume none of you have a knife, right?" Carter said not bothering to look up. There was a time we had knives, but those days were long gone. They'd been left behind, taken or lost.

The next time we found a place with supplies I made up my mind to look for a knife. That would be a tool that could come in handy in more ways than one. In fact, it was almost surprising Penn didn't have one hidden somewhere on his person.

Carter spent a solid fifteen minutes trying to make perfectly sculpted points for his fishing spear. He poked at one of them with his fingertip and quickly pulled it back. His lips curled up slowly at the ends, satisfied with their sharpness.

"Here goes nothing," he said walking over to the river and stepping on top of the rocks to get as close as he could without actually going in the water.

"See anything?" Alice shouted, but he waved at her in such a way that I knew he wanted to her be quiet. She rolled her eyes and hugged her knees. When she saw me watching her, she stared back at me awkwardly. I couldn't think of a single thing to say, so I quickly looked away trying to pretend I hadn't been looking at her. But we both knew I had been.

I got up and stood on a rock about five feet away from Carter. He held his spear just above the water and watched something moving below the surface. I wasn't sure if his plan was going to work or not but he stabbed quickly at the water.

When he frowned I knew he had missed it, but he adjusted the spear and jabbed it downward again. This time he held the spear down for a minute before raising it up to reveal a small fish that was just a bit bigger than my palm.

"Ah ha!" he said looking at me with a huge grin. It almost looked as though he had surprised himself.

"Now just do that a few more times," I said moving my fingers a few inches apart to show how small the fish was. It probably would have been impossible to even divide it up between everyone. One single bite per person. Of course, that was better than nothing, but it wouldn't be enough to survive on.

"Here," Carter said pulling the still wiggling fish off of his spear. He gripped it tightly and waved it in my direction. "Bring this to Penn."

"Ugh, do I have to?" I said taking several careful steps towards him and reaching out for the fish. I grabbed it not realizing exactly how feisty it would be, since it was the first time I'd held a dying fish. It was so wet and squirmy I had to hold on with both hands.

I carried it over to Penn and he looked at me like I was handing him a goldfish. Then he glanced over at Carter who was thrusting the spear back into the water. Penn shrugged and threaded a stick through the middle of the fish and placed it inside the flames.

Carter looked over his shoulder with a big smile on his face. He waved at me and I knew he'd caught another. What I wanted to know was how I had received the role of fish collector. I sighed, "Ugh, why me?"

Penn laughed. Sienna got up to stretch and quickly combed her hair with her fingers. She raised her hand up at me, "Don't worry... I'll help him."

"You got it," I said almost one hundred percent positive she had no idea he was about to hand her a half-dead fish. Penn met my eyes, and he chuckled, but it quickly faded. I couldn't even crack a smile because I could tell something was bothering Penn. "Want to talk about it?"

I moved over as close to him as I could, trying to block our conversation from Alice who seemed to be busy massaging her throat. Dean was off trying to find more of that wild spinach, but I wasn't sure he knew what he was looking for. He'd pick things up and look at them before throwing it back down on the ground.

"Talk about what?" Penn said raising his shoulder up as if to block me from seeing his face. I didn't need to see his face to know something was on his mind.

"You haven't seemed like yourself for awhile now and—"

"Ros, I don't even know myself. How can I

be myself when I don't know who I am?"

I squinted at him and shook my head, "I'm not sure what you mean…."

"It's like an ON switch has been flipped inside me since I left HOME. My brain is always on… like they made me this way. I'm always looking. I can barely sleep. I'm tired… no I'm fucking exhausted beyond comprehension. It doesn't stop, Ros! What did they do to me? Whatever it was I can't undo it!" he said with eyes so big I worried they might pop. His words had gotten so loud at the end that Alice glanced up towards us, but she wasn't freaking out so I figured she hadn't heard the part about HOME.

"You just need to relax. It's not your job to take care of everything," I said knowing how stupid my advice sounded as the words came out. But I didn't know the right things to say. I didn't know how to help him.

Penn laughed as if I'd said something funny. He shook his head as though I couldn't possibly understand, or maybe it was because he didn't know how to explain it. But in a way, I think I did understand. In a way I felt the same, although I'm not sure it was anywhere near the same extent that Penn felt it. It was like I was always trying to be aware. Always watching. Even when I was sleeping, it was with one eye open.

"I think if we can find a place to stay…," Penn said with a small glimmer of hopefulness in his eyes. He was seeing my vision of what Michigan could be.

"I think so too," I said with a nod. "We just

need to get somewhere we can feel safe again.
Well, a little safe anyway."

"But is it even possible?" he asked turning
and nodding at something behind me. Sienna was
making her way over to us holding onto another two
fish. She gripped one in each hand tightly, her face
scrunched up in utter disgust at what she was doing.

When she got closer, one of the fish leapt
out of her hand and she jumped away from it like
she was afraid it was going to attack her. Then she
quickly turned around to see if Carter was
watching. His back was to the camp, but she forced
herself to pick up the fish and hand it to Penn.

"Thanks," Penn said grabbing them and
spearing each with a stick. He placed them into the
fire next to the first.

"No problem," Sienna said wiping her hands
on her pants and then looking frustrated. "Ugh."

"That's what I thought too," I said with a
small smirk.

Penn removed the first fish from the fire. It
was charred, and the skin looked as though it was
peeling away from the meat. He held out the
bottom of the stick towards me as if he was passing
me a popsicle.

"I'll pass," I said even though my stomach
was incredibly angry with me. I was ravenously
hungry, but I'd much rather eat the random leaf
Dean would bring back, over forcing myself to gag
on the fish meat.

"Suit yourself," Penn said offering it to
Sienna. "Be careful. Don't eat the bones."

"I don't know how to…," Sienna said

looking at it as if she was trying to figure out what end to start at.

"Here, I'll help you," Penn said as he patted the ground next to him. I crossed my arms and wandered towards Dean to see if I could help with the gathering.

When I got closer, he abruptly spun around as if I had startled him. His hand was half way to the back of his waistband when he realized it was me.

"It's just me," I said with a smile.

"Lucky me," he said bending down to kiss me on the lips. He pressed his lips against mine and my body started to relax, but just for a moment until I remembered I couldn't.

"How's your arm?" I said lightly touching his arm below where his healing wound was.

"Better. Barely even notice it," he said with a smile so perfect I barely even remembered what I had asked him. I don't think I'd ever get used to just how gorgeous he was. Even out here in the middle of nowhere after everything, he still looked the way he did.

"They're having fish," I blurted out the first thing that popped into my head.

Dean looked up and over towards the campfire. He almost dropped all the leaves he'd collected when he saw Penn helping Sienna with the fish. Dean started to walk towards the camp as if his stomach had complete control of his body.

"Hey! I want those," I said narrowing my eyes at him. He stopped and took a small step backwards.

"Sure," he said pushing them against my body. He smiled, but then quickly walked away from me to get back over to the camp to stake his claim on some of the small fish. I shook my head at him, although I couldn't blame him. He was starving, just the same as the rest of us.

I knew I was stupid for not eating the fish, but if I'd just throw it up what was the point? This way at least they got to enjoy a little more of it. For now, I'd eat the leaves and hope we'd find some real food soon. We'd already walked for miles… chances were we'd find something.

I looked down at the leaves growing out of the ground and tried to match them up to the leaves Dean had given me. There seemed to be a decent amount growing around me. I'd find as much as I could, or at least that was what I thought before I heard the howl of the dog-beast in the distance. I tightly held onto the leaves Dean had gathered and jogged back to the group, not wanting to be alone if the dog-beast came our way.

* * *

After everyone finished eating their tiny fish, and I'd eaten every last leaf Dean had gathered, Penn kicked out the fire and we were on our way. We followed the river for a long while before it twisted back, practically in the direction we had just come from.

We'd have to choose to stay with the river

for a water source or go in the right direction and leave the river behind. If we stayed with the water it would mean we'd have to travel for an unknown amount of time in the wrong direction, but if we left the water behind no one knew when we'd find a drink again.

Penn laid out the options, and we took a vote. We all agreed to leave the water source behind. We couldn't risk traveling back and losing all the miles we'd put in when we were so tired. Not to mention we were all sick of walking. No one wanted to add extra miles and more time to our route.

We'd go east. Alice had refrained from voting. But it didn't matter, it had been unanimous, and we all knew that whatever Carter's vote was would count as two because it wasn't like she would vote against him.

We all took a final drink of the unpurified water and headed east. I couldn't even guess how many hours or miles we walked, but the whole day had come and gone by the time we saw the barely standing gas station on the outskirts of a small town come into view.

Chapter seven.

The small town was in shambles. Some of the houses were still intact but many of them looked as though they were falling apart piece by piece. The destruction had probably been due to the storms since the buildings appeared to have been in this condition for some time. The older buildings probably hadn't been built to survive the devastating storms.

Then again, the storms that had come through around here must not have been as strong as the ones that had gone through North Dakota. If they had been, there would have been nothing left. The tornadoes would have ripped this little town to shreds.

We went inside the gas station and no one was surprised to see that it had been cleaned out. Even the expired stuff that sometimes remained wasn't sitting on the shelves.

"Let's check in the back," Penn said nodding towards the door that would likely lead towards the offices and storage areas. Dean followed him through a rickety white door with a small window near the top.

I made my way over to the main window and looked out over the area that had once been a parking lot. It seemed like someone should keep watch… just in case.

They returned after a couple minutes. Dean caught my eye and shook his head. I knew they hadn't found anything. He stood next to me and put his arm around my shoulders.

"We'll find something here," he said trying to sound confident.

"Maybe," I said, feeling far less confident. It wasn't a very big town.

"Let's get out of here," Penn said walking past me and out the front door. He kept his hand on the handle of his gun even though there wasn't anyone out there.

"I think we'll have better luck searching the houses," Dean said nodding down the deserted street.

My clothes were itchy from being wet with the river water and then having dried while I wore them, but I didn't care about finding new clothes as much as I did finding water. And something to eat that would be better and more filling than wild spinach.

One of the houses had to have something. Anything. And if we couldn't find food or water, maybe we could find a car with a full tank of gas. Then we could just drive until we found something.

We started walking down the road and carefully went inside the first house on the first block we came upon. It had been completely stripped of anything that might have been useful. There wasn't anything left inside, those who'd come through had even destroyed the furniture.

"Not even a pot," I said opening the kitchen cabinets.

"Come on," Penn said throwing a piece of wood from the counter onto the floor. "There are other houses."

"What if they are all like this?" Sienna said hugging herself as if she was cold.

We left and continued walking down the block checking houses. With each one we got more and more discouraged. Our feet moved slower as we made our way through the neighborhood having found nothing we could use.

At the very least we'd be able to find a shelter, but we needed food and water. We really needed water. With all the walking we did, it didn't take long to feel in my mouth and throat how badly we needed the water.

"I'm so tired," Sienna said hanging her head forward.

"Me too," Alice mumbled as if she was afraid her opinion wouldn't matter. I glanced at her at the same time Carter did and I wondered if he noticed that she looked even more pale. He probably noticed every change even before I did, since he knew her far better than I.

Penn nodded and instead of turning towards the next closest house, he pointed to a house down the road. It was a bit separated from the city and surrounded by mostly dead trees and shrubbery.

"That one… over there," Penn said as he turned to lead the way. He climbed up the steps to the two-story house and looked around the area before he opened the creaky door.

"Why are you picking the haunted one?" I said trying to make a joke, but the house did have a somewhat eerie feeling.

"Because no one else is going to go to the haunted house," Penn said with a half-smile.

The house was encircled by the trees but they didn't provide much cover. If they'd been covered in green leaves, it would have been much more isolated. It would have been nicer to find somewhere more hidden because even though we hadn't seen the road pirates, or resistance, that didn't mean they weren't around. We couldn't afford to let our guard down.

I stepped inside the house after Penn and Dean. At first glance I could tell the house had been gone through, but it wasn't in quite the same condition the others had been in. Cabinet doors hadn't been ripped off their hinges and the owner's personal effects hadn't been strewn about.

It seemed as though most of the furniture had been taken, although the sofa remained. Whoever took them didn't want to bother carrying or hauling a large sofa. I wondered how close whoever had taken them was. Maybe they were just down the road in a house we hadn't gone inside, but maybe they were miles and miles away.

Dean, Penn and I looked upstairs while the others remained on the first floor. They were looking through the kitchen for things we could use while we continued through the house making sure it was empty.

There were two bedrooms upstairs. In the first there was a child's dresser, each drawer had been opened, and the clothing scattered around. The sheets had been pulled off of the mattress that was hanging halfway off of the box-spring.

In the next room the mattress was laying on the floor near the door. It appeared as though someone had tried to take it, but they gave up when it was either too heavy or they were having too much trouble getting it out of the bedroom door.

"Help me with this," Penn said, and Dean helped him put the mattress back on top of the box-spring.

"Why bother?" I said shrugging as I looked inside the dresser doors. If there had been clothing in the dresser drawer, they had been emptied. I guess I wasn't the only one out there looking for clean clothing.

There was probably two hundred dollars in twenty dollar bills scattered about inside the top dresser drawer. I found it somewhat amusing that money was completely useless. Someone would rather have clothing than two hundred dollars.

I opened the closet door and found clothes still hanging inside. Whoever had been in here had forgotten to check the closet, or maybe they had been in a hurry. Whatever the reason, I'd hopefully be able to find a change of clothing.

I moved things around looking to see if anything had been left behind that we could use. There was a large gaudy hat, a few belts with big buckles and a shoe box hidden behind a pile of books.

I slowly removed the lid of the shoe box like I was afraid it might explode if I moved too quickly. I grinned when I realized what I was looking at.

It was a box full with about twenty candy

bars packed neatly inside, and every single one of them was calling out to me. My mouth started to water. They most certainly weren't nutritious, but it was something. It wasn't just something, it was chocolate.

"You aren't going to believe this," I said trying to hide my excitement.

"What is it?" Penn said turning his head sharply as if he was afraid I'd found a poisonous snake.

I turned around and showed them the stockpile of candy bars. Dean smiled and took several quick steps towards me. He looked inside the box and ran his fingers over the slick wrappers. It was like he had to touch them to believe they were real.

"Hopefully, they found other things downstairs," Penn said as he gestured towards the door.

"What's better than chocolate?" I joked to Dean when Penn was out of earshot. Or at least I thought he had been.

"Food," Penn said over his shoulder. "Like actual real food."

"I don't remember what that is anymore," I said holding my candy bar box against my chest.

When we got downstairs, I was hoping to see a big pile of canned or prepackaged goods laid out on the table, but there wasn't. There was a can of chicken noodle soup and a box of dried noodles. I set down the shoe box without telling Sienna, Alice and Carter what was inside. If I told them I wasn't sure they'd wait until we figured out how we

were going to ration out the few things that had
been gathered.

Penn sighed as he opened a small door that
led to the garage. I followed him out and crossed
my fingers that we'd find a working car, but I
wasn't surprised when there wasn't one waiting for
us. All that was in the garage were molding two-
by-fours, a bike with two flat tires and other random
garage junk.

"Hey! A grill," Carter said as he started
moving towards it as if he was going to grill us up
some steaks. Maybe he was imagining the fish or
other wild animals we could cook on top of it, if we
had any.

He took about four steps before he tripped
over a board and fell. Carter stumbled towards the
garage's side wall. His hand stretched out and he
mostly caught himself, but stepped on a tarp which
slipped down and revealed a beautiful sight.

Sitting there on the floor were two giant jugs
of water. They were huge containers, the kind you
put in water dispensers, but that didn't matter. They
were filled with water, that's what mattered.

Penn smiled, "I think I could kiss you right
now."

"You don't have to," Carter said as his lips
curled upwards. He knelt down and examined the
top of one of the jugs. "Was there one of those
things inside to put this on?"

"Hmm... I didn't see one," Penn said
hovering over Carter's shoulder. "We don't need
one. Get some cups."

I ran to the kitchen and looked through the

cabinets for something we could drink out of. Everything had been taken except for a single hard water stained plastic cup that had a crack in it. It would have to do.

When I went back inside the garage, they were all staring at me. They didn't look thrilled when they saw me standing there with a single cup. I shrugged, "It was all that was left."

I handed it to Penn who held the cup while Dean and Carter tried to carefully fill it with water. They had trouble pouring the water at first. It all spilled out around the cup until they figured out how to manage the large jug. We all looked at the filled cup as if it was sacred.

"Go get Sienna and Alice," Penn said as he lifted the cup and placed it against his lips. He closed his eyes as he slowly drank the water. His slow sips quickly turned into big gulps and in seconds he had the cup back on the garage floor waiting to be refilled. Dean and Carter worked to fill it, spilling less this time than they had the first time.

I was grinning from ear to ear as I practically danced back inside the house to get Sienna and Alice. They weren't in the kitchen so I went towards the living room calling out for them.

"We're in here," Sienna said as I turned the corner. Alice was laying down on the sofa hugging her knees loosely up towards her chest. Sienna was sitting on the floor with her legs crossed looking down at her fingers. She looked up at me, "I wish we had some medicine for her."

"Me too, but we did find water," I said, but

my smile faded. Alice started coughing, and I
watched her body jerk forward with each one. She
didn't bother to cover her mouth. It seemed as
though she didn't have the energy, or maybe she
had just forgotten. "I'll get her some water."

I dashed back out to the garage and I could
tell by the looks on their faces that they'd all
already had taken their turn at the drinking cup.
Penn handed me the full cup, and I was about to
take it to Alice when I stopped and drank from the
uncontaminated cup.

"Alice needs water," I said taking a small
break, "but we can't share a cup… can we? I mean
we shouldn't, right?"

Penn glanced at Carter as if he might have
the answer. Carter shrugged, "I've been around her
this long and still haven't caught the cold."

"Yes," Dean said, and I knew he was
thinking about Sienna's well-being. "Bring Sienna
a drink first, then come back for more. Maybe we
can find something in here we can use for Alice."

The boys started looking around the garage
and I left to bring Sienna her water. I told Alice I'd
bring hers next. She blinked weakly at me and I
was pretty sure she knew why she would be
drinking last.

When I went back out to the garage, they
had found and cleaned out an old coffee mug. It
was filled and ready for me to bring to Alice. I
rushed it back inside and helped her drink.

"I just need to catch up on rest, and then I'll
be fine," she said giving up the fight to keep her
eyes open.

"Ok," I said and set the mug down on the floor next to the sofa. They boys were noisily hauling the water jug inside, but their racket didn't seem to bother her in the least.

After we each had a drink from the canned soup and a candy bar, we took turns looking through the upstairs closet for anything that we could change into. I exchanged my shirt for a clean one, but there weren't any pants that would fit me so I had to keep the stiff, itchy pair I'd worn for far too long.

"We should probably all stay upstairs," Penn said as he walked from window to window scanning the area for anything out of the ordinary. "I think it'll be safer."

"But she's asleep," Carter said and I could tell he didn't want to disturb her. She needed her rest.

"Can you carry her? It'll be safer up there for all of us," Penn said without looking away from the front window.

Carter didn't answer but bent down and scooped her up off of the bed and headed upstairs. I followed as Penn and Dean went through the downstairs checking to make sure all the doors and windows were locked. After a few minutes I heard them stomping up the steps. They were working together to bring the water jug upstairs. Sienna followed them carrying the cups.

Carter had lowered Alice onto the smaller bed. He stood in the doorway as if blocking our entrance into the room. She moaned and then rolled over onto her other side.

"Come in here with us... let her rest," Sienna said lightly tugging on his sleeve. "She'll be OK in there. If anyone came up inside we'd hear them."

Carter glanced back at his sister and then followed Sienna into the larger bedroom. It was obvious how much he cared about his sister. Just like Dean and Sienna.

Penn sat by the window in a chair that had a broken armrest. Dean and I sat on the bed. Carter glanced at the door but then slid down to the floor and stared at his feet. Sienna lowered herself down next to him and smiled.

"Well take turns keeping watch out of this window," Penn said mostly for Carter's ears, but after our night at the river he probably already had how we did things all figured out. "I'll go first."

Dean tossed Sienna one of the two flat pillows and a ripped up blanket. I laid down on the mattress and felt instantly warmer when Dean laid down behind me. He wrapped his arm around my waist and I smiled.

I closed my eyes and tried to sleep, but as I often did, I struggled to relax my body. Sleep wasn't finding me as easily as I had hoped it would.

Sienna was whispering something to Carter. I watched them between the narrow slits of my semi-closed eyes. Every once in a while a smile would appear on one of their faces and I knew what was happening.

I knew she had felt it practically the minute she saw him, but now I saw he felt it too. His smile would fade and he'd turn towards the door every time the bed in the other room squeaked or creaked, but once it settled again, his attentions would return to Sienna.

The last thing I saw happen before sleep finally found me, was Carter twining his dirty fingers into Sienna's equally dirty fingers. They couldn't hold one another's eyes for long before they'd look away with big smiles on their faces. It was obvious... they had it bad.

I wasn't sure how long I had been asleep when I woke up to the smell of smoke.

Chapter eight.

I had been dreaming. I was inside a large building and was walking down a long, dark, empty hallway. The feeling of aloneness was so strong that after I had woken it still lingered.

In the dream I walked past rooms, each one containing something different. Some of them I couldn't see inside, but I still knew that what was inside of them was scary. Not something I even wanted to see, necessarily.

One of the rooms was filled with doctors and nurses moving around. I couldn't see the patient, but I knew they were preforming surgery. I could see the patient's unmoving feet. Then one of the nurses pushed the door, and it swung shut.

At the next room, the door had been open just a crack and I could hear the whispers of the people inside. It was like they were talking another language. None of it made any sense.

Before I could look inside the next door, I saw an orange glow coming from the last room at the end of the hallway. I ran towards it, sensing someone was inside and needed help.

When I looked inside the door, Seth was standing there smiling at me as the fire surrounded him. I started to back away as his flaming body moved closer to me. My back was against the wall as he stopped in the doorway and stared out at me.

I wanted to scream but I couldn't. My lungs felt like they were filled with smoke and I felt like I was struggling to take in a breath. That's when I must have woken up, because I was staring at the walls trying to make sense of where I was and gasping for air. I could still smell the smoke lingering in the air.

I saw Penn sleeping in his chair and I knew I wasn't in the cold building with the strange rooms any more. I remembered we were in some random house, but I couldn't shake the sense something wasn't right.

I sat up and looked around the room. Everyone was still asleep and there was a strange yellow and orange glow that flickered and danced on the walls. What was going on?

"Penn!" I whispered loudly, but when he didn't answer I forced myself to get up and look out the window even though I felt scared. I pressed my palms against my scalp hard. It was like I wanted to make sure I wasn't still dreaming. Outside of the house, all the dead trees and shrubbery that surrounded us were engulfed in flames.

It crossed my mind, if only for a second, that maybe I should just go back to bed and let this be the end. I was tired. All we every did was fight and struggle, and maybe I was ready to be done with it. But I shook the thought away. Even if I could make that choice for myself, I couldn't do that for the others. It just wasn't my call.

I shook Penn awake, and he looked at me with wide, unblinking eyes. He stared at me as if he had no idea who I was.

"Look!" I said, pointing out the window towards the burning trees. He blinked hard several times and rubbed his eyes before he turned to the window.

"Oh, shit!" he said standing up so fast he knocked the chair over onto its side. The noise caused the others to stir.

"What's going on?" Sienna said with a yawn.

Dean swung his legs over the side of the bed and rushed to the window. He looked around the room, "Is the house on fire too? I smell smoke!"

"I don't think so. The smell is just slowly filling the house," I said, even though I wasn't completely sure the house wasn't on fire. But it seemed like a fair assumption, considering the amount of grass, between the house and the trees, that wasn't in flames. At least for now it was just the surrounding trees and shrubs, but it would eventually take over the house as well.

"So are we surrounded?" Dean said glancing towards Sienna, noticing how close she was to Carter. He kept his eyes on them until Carter stood up and came to look out the window. Sienna narrowed her eyes at Dean and crossed her arms.

"I think so," I said watching the fire outside the window get bigger and brighter. I looked down at my feet, hoping that when I looked back up the fire would be gone. But it wasn't. And if we didn't do something soon, we'd be cooked alive. "Someone go get Alice?"

"I'll wake her," Carter said, and disappeared from the room.

"The water," Penn said solemnly as he looked at the water. He walked over to the jug and started filling the glass as if it might be the last time he'd see water.

"Penn, we have to get out of here," Dean said pulling on Penn's shirt. Penn chugged down the water and dropped the cup as he reluctantly left the jug of water behind. It was far too heavy and bulky. We wouldn't have been able to carry it easily. It would have slowed us all down too much.

"There's time! We should each have one more glass," Penn said pulling himself away and moving back towards the jug. I could see the flames rising up in the trees. The blazing limbs looked like fiery beasts reaching out their arms towards us.

"There's no time!" Dean said as Carter and Alice joined us in the hallway. Dean walked around me to go back for Penn.

Alice looked frightened. It almost looked as though she thought she was dreaming. Carter held onto her tightly, as if he was afraid she might run away.

We walked down the hall and Dean stopped at the window. He pointed down at the ground, "Look!"

I looked over his shoulder and saw what appeared to be a shadowy figure running away from the fire. It looked as though he was carrying something. Something like a gas can.

"What the…? Why would someone do this?" I asked quietly. Yeah, people were jerks, but usually they ruined your day because they wanted your supplies, not because they wanted to set you on fire for fun.

"What did you see?" Sienna asked as she grabbed onto the railing and walked down the stairs.

Dean shook his head as if he wasn't sure he'd even seen it, "It looked like a person... maybe... I'm not sure. We need to get out of here."

"Ugh! I could have had like six glasses of water by now," Penn complained as Dean practically pulled him along. I followed behind, half expecting Penn to burst free and run back to the jug of water.

They had struggled to get the water up the stairs, I knew it wasn't feasible to carry it along. The heat from the fire might melt the plastic anyway. It just wasn't something we could manage in our condition. We could barely carry ourselves in our weakened state.

Once we were outside I saw how bad things really were. The smoke was thick in the heavy air and I could feel the heat the minute we stepped outside. The burning trees were almost a perfect circle around us.

"What are we going to do?" I asked coughing as the smoke entered my lungs. Sweat started to drip down my forehead, and I felt as though I was being cooked.

Penn's instincts finally kicked in and he started looking around. "Over there... there is a small break in the flames. I think we can get through."

I looked over to where he indicated but I didn't see what he saw. All I saw were hot flames jutting out from everywhere. There was no break in the flames anywhere that I could tell.

Penn faced the burning trees, "Here's what we are going to do—"

"Maybe we should go back inside and douse ourselves with water first," Carter said his eyes darting around from Alice to the fire to the house.

"There's no time for that. And probably not enough water for everyone anyway," Penn said quickly. He got down and pressed his palms to the ground. "Everyone down to the ground. As low as you can get and still move quickly. Hold your shirt over your nose and mouth like this," he said pulling his shirt upwards to demonstrate.

Dean looked at me and I shook my head side to side, "Are you sure about this?"

"Do exactly as I do and you'll be fine. Stay low. Move fast. It's going to be very hot," Penn warned as he crouched lower and started to maneuver his way between the branches. "Let's go!"

Dean took a breath and got down just as low as Penn had. He looked at me and then Sienna, "Follow right behind me."

Once he was moving, I nudged Sienna forward and gestured for her to go. She glanced back at Carter but then turned to follow Dean. I crouched down and followed her, maybe even too closely.

I could hear crunching as someone walked behind me. If I had to guess, it was probably Alice behind me and Carter behind her. The sweat poured off of my face as I made my way through.

I was about halfway when I knew I was going to make it alive. The noise of a tree branch cracking nearby startled me but not enough to stop me. I could feel a whoosh of hot air pass by as it fell towards the ground, missing us by a foot or two. We were lucky it didn't fall in front of us and trap us inside the trees. We would have been cooked to death in minutes.

Sienna stood up and started running from the trees. Even though there was smoke around I knew she was out in the clear. It would only be a few more steps and I could run for it too. I may have been cooked medium-rare, but that was far better than being well done… or burnt.

When I stood up my leg cramped and I stumbled to the side. The only thing there to stop myself from falling face first in the flames was a branch burning so hot it crackled.

My hand automatically grabbed onto it so I could steady myself. I wanted to scream, but I couldn't. My mouth opened, but nothing came out. I quickly pulled back my hand but the sleeve of my shirt caught fire.

"Ahhh! Help me!" I shouted as I moved towards the others with the flames dancing on my arm. I stopped when I saw the looks on their faces. I couldn't think straight. My arm was so hot. The skin felt like it was tightening and any minute it would just pop open and melt.

Dean stepped towards me and started swatting at my arm but it didn't help. He was burning his hand trying to save me and with each swat the panicked expression on his face scared me more and more.

"Get down!" Penn shouted as launched himself at me and tackled me to the ground. He pushed and rolled me around while he scooped up dirt and threw it at my arm.

"Ohhh nooo," I said. My eyes felt wet. I was either crying or sweating so badly it was dripping into my eyes. None of what was happening felt real. The world around me started to spin and fade away. "I can't…."

* * *

I must have passed out because we were a fair distance from the burning trees. It felt like I was in a dream but then, when the searing pain reminded me what had happened, I knew it hadn't been.

"Owww!" I cried out, afraid to look in the direction of my own arm. I held it out away from me as if I didn't want it any more. What I wanted right now was a new arm. This one was ruined.

It felt like someone was holding it. I could hear their voices. Someone asked if it was bad. Another said to rip the fabric of my shirt away. A third, in a hushed voice which almost magically seemed amplified, asked if the shirt was burned into my flesh.

"I can hear you!" I said pounding my good fist against my thigh. If I could make my leg hurt, maybe I'd stop thinking about my cooked arm.

"I can get it off," Penn said softly, and I wasn't sure if he was talking about the shirt or my arm.

"Take it off!" I shouted, and I meant my arm.

Dean was crouched down in front of me. He raised my chin up so I was forced to look into his eyes. He moved his mouth and instead of hearing his voice it felt like I was lip reading him, "Ros, it's not as bad as you think."

"It's not that bad?" I asked grimacing. "It hurts like hell!"

He half-smiled as he stroked my cheek with his thumb, "Oh, I believe you, but it's just bright red. No blisters, no broken skin… Penn got it out quick enough."

"No blisters yet," I said feeling my eyes fill up with water. I wasn't sure if I felt relieved by the news or if everything was just overwhelming. The skin felt tight and hot… it had to be worse than what he was telling me.

I closed my eyes hoping it would help me focus, but all I could think about was the pain from my elbow down to my wrist. I felt the cool tears leak out of the corners of my eyes and run down the side of my face.

"You're going to be fine," Penn said as I heard the ripping of another shirt. I wanted to scream when I felt the cloth touch my burned skin. Penn was trying to carefully wrap it around, but it was close to torture.

"No! Stop! You're killing me!" I shouted at him. I tried to swat at him with my other arm but I couldn't get it anywhere near him.

"I'm trying to help you. This will protect it. If it blisters you definitely do not want to get infected," Penn said as he tucked the end of the fabric inside itself. "We're going to have to find something better than that, but it'll do for now."

I tried to stand up, but I had trouble getting myself upright using just my good arm. Dean grabbed me and pulled me to my feet. He held onto me as if he was afraid I'd tip over … and maybe I would have.

"What do we do now?" Sienna asked looking at the house, which was now also covered in flames. If we would have stayed inside, we would have died.

Penn followed her gaze and shook his head. "Ros I'm so sorry," he said taking my good hand into his. His eyes were glassy.

"For what?"

"If I hadn't fallen asleep… your arm. This is all my fault," Penn said with his shoulders slumped forward. He blamed himself. None of this was his fault. He needed a break more than any of us. If he didn't get one soon, I wasn't sure if he'd be OK. Penn needed to be able to slow down and catch his breath. More than ever I wanted us to hurry up and get to our destination.

I could feel the adrenaline surge through my body. I didn't know if it was from everything that just happened or my desire to get us to Michigan. Whatever the reason, it dulled the pain, and I was more determined than ever to get us to our new place. It would be there waiting for us.

It would have plenty of water from a nearby lake. We'd be able to grow food and catch fish. Best of all, it would be safe. We wouldn't have to worry and everything would finally be OK. All we had to do was get there.

"It's not your fault," I said smiling as I squeezed his hand. He forced a brief smile, and I knew he would blame himself no matter what I said. "Let's go to town and find a car. There has to be one somewhere."

"What if we run into that guy Dean saw out the window? The one that started the fire?" Sienna asked as if she was worried we might be walking right into a trap.

"I'm not worried," Penn said patting his gun in his waistband to indicate what he'd do if he ran into a guy with a gas can.

He touched his hand against his forehead and took a deep breath. It was like he pressed a button somewhere inside himself that would make him go, even when he was too tired to move. He pushed his shoulders back and raised his head. "Let's move."

Chapter nine.

We picked the first house we saw that we hadn't already been inside. Penn slowly led the way through the house. I was worried that someone was hiding around every corner we turned. It was like I could already see them dousing us in gasoline and lighting the match that would finish what they had started.

It wasn't just me though, everyone seemed a touch more on edge because of the person Dean and I saw leaving the scene of the fire. If we ran into one person, Penn would easily manage it, but what if we ran into a whole group of fire-starting lunatics?

Once the house was cleared, we broke off looking for food and water, but no one found anything. I was kicking myself for not grabbing the box of chocolate bars as we left the last house. Although, with the heat from the fire, they surely would have melted.

I lightly ran my fingers across the cloth bandage Penn had wrapped around my arm. The sting reminded me of the whole ordeal.

"You OK?" Dean asked looking at my arm as though he was worried something was wrong.

"Yeah… it hurts but I'll live."

"Not the burn, you. Are you OK?" Dean said putting his arm around my shoulder.

I shook my head side-to-side. After everything we'd been through I wasn't going to let a burn stop me, but I did feel emotionally and physically drained. I bit my lip so I wouldn't cry. It wouldn't be a cry of sadness or weakness, but a cry of frustration and exhaustion. I turned away from him, "Yeah. Yeah... I'm fine."

Penn found himself a new shirt and a closet full of hoodies. He offered them to anyone who might want one and everyone took one. Whoever had lived here before seemed to have collected them. There was one in every color and some colors had multiples. It was only too bad he hadn't collected bottled water and snack bars.

The house had pretty much been emptied, but there was one thing that hadn't been taken. Sitting in the garage was a car covered in a thin layer of dust. Even though most of my thoughts were on the pain I was in, I couldn't help but smile at the car. To me, the car meant life. Well, if we could find the keys and gas for it then we'd live another day.

"Look everywhere and anywhere for the keys," Penn said as his eyes settled on my arm. He grabbed my good hand and pulled me back inside the house. "Let's see if we can find a better bandage."

Everyone went off in different directions to do different tasks. Dean, Sienna and Alice went in search of the keys. First, they looked in the garage, but then I could hear them inside the house. I was sitting on the lid of the toilet while Penn dug around in the bathroom cabinets.

He pulled out some extremely expired antibiotic cream, medical tape that had little threads running through it lengthwise, and a towel from the drawer that looked clean. He unscrewed the cap from the cream and set the tube down on the counter.

Penn put his fingertips inside the cloth wrapped around my arm and carefully removed it. I tried not to look, but at the same time it was like a car accident. I couldn't help but want to see the damage that had been done to my arm.

It wasn't nearly as bad as I expected it would be. I imagined it was going to be bloody with chunks of skin peeling away and blisters the size of grapes, but it wasn't that bad.

There was a large part of the side of my arm from elbow to wrist that was bright red. There wasn't any blood, blisters or peeling, but it was far worse than any sunburn I'd ever seen.

"Oh," I said looking at the redness.

"Hmm?"

"It's not as bad as I thought it'd be," I said as I wiggled my fingers and winced. When I moved, it felt like the skin was being pulled tighter which caused me extra pain.

Penn smiled briefly but turned serious again when he was about to squeeze some of the cream onto his fingertips. He stopped and started looking around.

"What is it?"

"My hands. They are too dirty. I don't want to….," Penn said pulling out a washcloth from the drawer. "This will do."

He squeezed out a dollop of the cream onto the corner of the washcloth and gently dabbed it on my burn. At first it stung but then the cooling effect kicked in and it actually started to soothe the burn.

"It's not as bad as I thought it would be either," he said as he made sure he got cream on all of the red areas. "A bad first-degree burn I think."

"It may not look bad, but it hurts. It hurts like hell," I said as he draped the bigger clean towel on top of the cream and started taping it down on my arm. He used a lot of tape but I knew it was because he didn't want it to fall off.

"You'll probably want to hold it still as much as you can. Honestly though, I have no idea how to treat or care for a burn," Penn said standing back and looking at his bandaging job. He raised an eyebrow and lowered his head.

"It's not the best bandage I've seen, but it'll do. And for what it's worth it does feel better," I said smiling up at him. "Take that cream with."

Penn nodded and shoved it inside his pocket. He reached out his hand to me and helped me up. "Let's see if they found the keys."

I followed him out to the living room where Dean was packing. Sienna was sitting on the sofa resting her chin on her palm while Alice sat rocking back and forth in a chair coughing softly.

"No keys I take it?" I said, already pretty sure I knew the answer.

Alice shook her head, but grinned when the rumble of the car engine filled the air. Carter must have found the keys and started the car. I had worried that maybe the car wouldn't start considering how long it had sat there unused, but it was running. It was loud, but the important part was that it worked.

We all dashed out to the garage. Carter was standing there leaning against the car with his arms crossed in front of his chest. He was grinning from ear to ear.

"You found the keys!" I said walking over towards him and patting him on the arm. I was already imagining us sitting inside and heading towards our new home in Michigan.

"Nope," Carter said with a smirk.

"Then how?" I said looking inside the windows and coming up with our seating chart for the most comfortable ride. Now that there were two more of us, it would be a bit tighter of a fit than we were used to. And I'd need somewhere to put my burned arm so it didn't get squished. If only we would have found another SUV, or van.

Penn started digging around the garage. He threw things around until he pulled up a scummy, tangled up, green hose with a yellow stripe running down lengthwise. After he cut it down with a rusty handsaw, he threw it in the back of the car.

"I know a little trick or two," Carter said opening the driver side door and offering it to Penn.

He nodded and climbed inside as he waved for everyone to get in. I was pretty sure he was in a hurry to get out of this little town. Or maybe it was the loudness of the car that made him nervous. It was possible that it could draw unwanted attention.

If the road pirates were nearby they'd come running, although this time we had nothing for them to steal. Although they would likely take the hose and the gas from the car.

"You hot-wired it? How do you know how to do that?" Penn asked as Carter lowered himself into the seat behind Penn. Alice, Sienna, and I walked around to the other side and Sienna slipped in first. She scooted all the way over so that she was right up against Carter and he smiled as he stretched his arm up around the back of the seat behind her.

Alice turned to look at me and rolled her eyes. I didn't know if she didn't like Sienna or if she just didn't like the idea of some girl hanging all over her brother. That was probably a feeling Sienna could relate to, not that I really ever hung all over Dean.

"I did," Carter said as if he was proud of his wiring skills. "I may have gotten into some trouble back in the day. Learned a few things."

"Well, lucky for us you were a troublemaker, I guess," Dean said shooting a quick glance at his sister. He sat down in the passenger seat and clicked his seatbelt into place. He hit the door a couple of times with the side of his fist anxious to get out of here.

Once we were all inside, Penn shifted the car in reverse and drove us out of the garage. In minutes we were back out on the road looking for the highway. And hopefully somewhere we could stop for food and water.

"We should have probably looked through the house better," I said once we were at least a few miles away. It had been pretty cleaned out but there probably would have been something we could have taken.

My fingers rubbed against the soft pile of the towel taped to my arm. Before we left the house it hadn't really crossed my mind to dig around for things that might be of use. I had been far too anxious to get inside the car and out of that town. I wanted to get to our destination and maybe the others' thoughts had been the same.

"We'll stop the first chance we get," Penn said, but he probably thought we'd made a mistake too. Maybe we could have found matches, or a pot to boil water in… little things we could have put to some kind of use. But there would be more houses, shops and gas stations.

Once we found our way to the interstate, we realized how off course we'd gotten by not following the roads. It took a few hours for us to get back on track. We stopped at every gas station or market we came across along the way, but everything had been cleaned out. Even though we hadn't come across other people or cars traveling down the road, the area must have been busy at one point or another since there wasn't anything left.

We weren't desperate yet, but I knew how badly we needed water. And the others knew it too. Thankfully we covered far more area in a car than we could on foot.

"We always stop at gas stations and grocery stores," Alice said tapping her chin. It looked as though she had an idea, but that she wasn't sure about it. "Why don't we try looking somewhere else. Maybe something no one else has thought of yet."

I looked at her and raised my eyebrow, "Like where?"

"How about a hotel? Or maybe an office building… a restaurant?" Alice said looking out of the window at our passing surroundings.

There weren't any hotels, offices or restaurants in this area. The only thing around us was rocky, hilly terrain and distant mountains.

"Gas stations are always easy to find along the highways," Penn said as if he was trying to explain why we usually stuck to gas stations. They were quick and easy stops, but now we were running out of options. For miles and miles, anything that was accessed easily off of the main roads had been emptied out a long time ago. Or so it seemed. It was time to try other places, even if there were more risks involved. "OK. Next town, we'll check something different."

Alice nodded and smiled. But her pleased expression of feeling helpful quickly vanished when she coughed into her hand. She saw me looking at her and quickly turned her head away from me.

I wasn't exactly sure how long we had been driving, but it felt like a long time. With how frequently Penn looked down at the dash, I knew we needed to find gas, and soon.

We had the hose for siphoning, but first we needed to find cars that still had gas. If we didn't find something we'd be without a car once again, and I was sure none of us wanted that. We covered so many more miles in the car than we could on foot.

~ Running Away ~

I could feel the shift in everyone's mood when the distant buildings came into view. After countless miles we were finally approaching a city.

Chapter ten.

Penn slowed the car as we passed the green sign that hung on a lone post marking the exit to the city. The bullet holes in the sign made me nervous. I didn't mention it, but Penn had probably noticed them too.

He turned down the exit and drove slowly towards the city. Most of the buildings we passed looked like they were falling apart. The storms had probably weakened them, but time was making them worse. Some of the buildings looked as though strips of wood had been carefully removed… repurposed for some reason or another.

"There," Alice said pointing at a building that had clearly been a motel at one time. The sign was covered in dirt, but I could still make out the name of the chain. As we drove closer, I worried the building might fall on top of us if we went inside. I couldn't tell for sure but the building looked as though it was tilting ever so slightly to the side.

Some of the windows were coated with a brown, dusty layer of dried muck and others were cracked or broken. There were brown and green vines trying to climb the walls. It looked like the earth was going to swallow it whole.

Penn pulled into the parking lot and slowly drove around the building. When no one came out, or started shooting at us through the broken windows, he pulled into one of the many empty parking spots.

Penn looked down at the wires, "How do I turn off the car? Should I turn off the car?"

"Yeah… just disconnect those wires. Let me show you," Carter said and got out of the car. He showed Penn how to start and stop the car by touching or disconnecting the wires.

Dean watched and nodded as Penn tried to start and stop the car without Carter's help. They smiled as though they'd just learned a magician's secrets.

Penn took out his gun from behind his back and checked it over. It reminded me we needed to find ammunition, and soon.

"Let's go," he said, and Carter stepped to the side so Penn could open his car door. We all got out and followed him up to the hotel door. It was the kind of door a keycard was typically needed to access, but Penn easily pulled the door open. The system had probably been disabled long ago.

He entered the hallway slowly shifting his gun from doorway to doorway. Dean took out his gun but kept it down by his thigh. I didn't bother to take mine out. I didn't have the speed or accuracy that would be needed if someone stepped out. Thinking about the gun only reminded me of what happened when I last used it. I was worried that if I touched it, visions of killing Ryan would flood back.

"Eww," Sienna said as she tip-toed around behind me.

"Tell me about it," I mumbled as I looked around at the black splotches on the walls.

There were all sorts of things scattered on the floor... broken picture frames, mud, pamphlets, possibly dead mice, and other random things I couldn't identify. In the corner of the entrance way there was a plant in a giant pot. Its leaves and vines twisted around the ground and up the walls. I had no idea what kind of plant it was, but for some reason it was thriving.

I looked up towards the ceiling and spotted an area above the plant that looked as though water had leaked through. Perhaps any time it rained, the plant got a drink. Then all it would need was some sunlight to come in through what remained of the glass door. The plant was a fighter... or maybe it was just lucky.

As I looked around I couldn't decide if the hotel had been ransacked or if it had just been messed up from the storms that had likely passed through forever ago. The ceiling was spotted with mold and mildew, and dirt coated the floors. If there had been people rummaging around inside, I would have thought there would be less dirt and maybe even footprints.

Once we got closer to where the front lobby was, Penn started pushing at doors to see if they'd swing open. He found the office, a maintenance closet and a room that stored all the still perfectly folded bed linens and towels.

"We should take some of those," Penn said, and I reached inside the closet and grabbed a stack of the towels. I winced at the stinging twinges of my burned skin feeling as though it was being stretched out.

Once we were in the lobby, I was sure people had come inside the hotel at some point. Most of the chairs were missing, leaving markings on the floor where they had once been, and there were footprints all around the area.

We continued onward to what had been a small cafe area. There were some cabinets under the counters and I opened them to see if anything was still inside. Most everything had been taken except for some sugar and sugar substitute packets, and a big stack of Styrofoam cups still wrapped in protective plastic.

I pulled them out and handed the stack to Sienna. We could definitely put the cups to use.

"Take that too," Penn said nodding towards a large plastic pitcher that probably had been used to make fancy blended coffee drinks or cold fruit smoothies. What I wouldn't give for a cold smoothie.

Sienna grabbed the pitcher and looked inside. She quickly pulled her head away and scrunched up her nose. The pitcher probably hadn't been cleaned out in quite some time. It might be so bad that we couldn't even use it, but she took it anyway.

"Follow," Penn said, and led us back down the hallway to the other end of the hotel. We walked maybe ten feet before Penn turned into a small square room.

He tucked his gun into the back of his pants and placed his hands against the sides of the vending machine. He started shaking the machine vigorously.

At first I wasn't sure what he was doing, but when I stepped to the side, I could see the machine was filled with snacks. Once he stopped shaking it, he started to pound his fist against the glass or plastic or whatever it was that was keeping us from the glorious snacks. Dean grabbed his hand and stopped him before he injured himself.

"Let's think before you break your hand," Dean said trying to look into Penn's eyes. It was like he was possessed by the need for food and it wasn't his brain that was making choices, it was his stomach. "There has to be something we can use instead of your fists."

"I have an idea... hold on," Carter said waving his hand at us as he walked away from us backwards. He jogged down the hallway, and I watched as he opened the maintenance closet. He stepped inside for less than a minute and popped back out carrying a hammer. As he drew closer, he raised it up and pointed at it, "Ta-da!"

He motioned for everyone to step aside and once we were all clear he swung the hammer hard towards the front of the vending machine. It cracked, and he sent the hammer flying towards it again, aiming for the exact same spot he'd hit the first time.

The hammer went through and made a small hole. Carter used the back of the hammer to knock away the loose shards before stepping aside to allow Penn to access the array of snacks.

Penn grabbed a bag of chips and tore it

open. He put them into his mouth three or four at a time as he stepped back to let everyone else have a turn.

Everyone grabbed something different and when we finished our first package, we all started on another and then another. I was nowhere near full or satisfied, but it was about a thousand times better than the feeling of my stomach gnawing on itself.

"We should take the rest of this with us. Even rationed, this probably won't last long," I said, causing the smiles to fade from everyone's faces as they remembered our bleak situation.

"She's right," Penn said looking around the area. "We're going to need a bag or something."

"Maybe there are trash bags in the closet," Carter said making his way back towards it. "That could work."

"Check behind the counter, they might have medicine back there," I said when Alice coughed behind me. Even if there wasn't any cold medicine, they'd probably have pain relievers and other over-the-counter medicines that could come in handy.

"You know what?" Penn said looking around the corner. "I bet they have a vending machine on the second floor too."

We finished clearing out the hotel of everything we could find. Sienna carried the hammer and Carter carried the garbage bag filled with all of our collected supplies... the towels, the random sugar packets, the plastic pitcher, the Styrofoam cups and the medicines Carter had found. And most importantly, the snacks.

After we had finished going over the second floor, I noticed through a window that the sunlight was starting to fade. It seemed as though the days were going quicker and quicker which I assumed meant summer would soon come to an end.

As long as we made it to Michigan, found a place and made it safe before winter came I figured we'd be in good shape. But if we didn't make it somewhere before the snow started to fall, I wasn't sure we'd survive wandering around in the wilderness.

Then again, I was only speculating that it would be fall soon. We could have months before the weather would turn cooler. Ever since the very first storms hit and took away everything we had ever known, the climate seemed to have been affected. I didn't even know what season it really was, the best any of us could do was guess.

I'd went through winter in Alaska and then we traveled around in what felt like spring. Now the weather was warmer and it only made sense that it was summer and fall would come next.

"It'll be night soon," Penn said looking around at each one of us. "We can stay here the night or drive through hoping to find gas somewhere."

"Stay here," Dean said with a shrug.

"Drive through the night," I answered at nearly the same time. I looked at him, "We need to find water."

"We need sleep too," Dean countered.

"We can sleep in the car… take turns. We'll make progress if we drive through the night," I said as if trying to convince him. Dean rubbed his chin and then nodded.

"Anyone else have a vote?" Penn asked looking around, but no one said anything. It didn't seem to matter too much.

"All right. Let's go then," Dean said, and Penn led us back out towards the car. I didn't say anything, but I was worried the car wouldn't be out there when we got back downstairs. We left the hotel in the same way we'd entered and I smiled when I saw the car still there waiting for us.

If we would have stayed the night at the hotel who knows if it would have still been there in the morning? Or maybe someone would have come and set the whole hotel on fire while we were inside.

Carter stuffed the garbage bag of supplies into the trunk and we all climbed back into the car. Penn tried to get it started again, and on the third try the engine roared.

"I can drive," Dean offered. Penn had done all the driving since we'd found the car and he probably could have used a break.

"I'm fine," Penn said putting the car into reverse. He barely glanced behind him as he drove the car backwards. He jerked it into drive and hit the gas, "We'll switch soon."

And with that we were back on the road. Instead of driving back towards the highway he turned towards town.

"It's going to be dark. We should get out of the city... go back to the highway," I said leaning forward to make sure he heard me.

"I need bullets," he said, and I realized why he wanted to drive. Dean wouldn't have agreed to this. He would have turned back towards the highway.

"What if we can't find a place… or what if there isn't any? We don't know our way around! Please Penn! You can have my gun," I said taking it out of my waistband and thrusting it towards him.

He raised his shoulder blocking me from passing it to him. Penn groaned and slammed his palms against the steering wheel before he made a quick U-turn. I sat back and let the wave of relief wash over me.

Penn knew better. It seemed like he wasn't thinking clearly. For him to want to drive us into the unknown darkness just didn't make any sense. He must have been really desperate for ammo because he would have known the potential risks involved in his plan. They weren't worth it. It just didn't seem like him and then it hit me.

"How long have you been out of bullets?" I asked crossing my arms in front of me. It was probably something I should have confronted him on in private, but I couldn't stop myself. I wanted him to know he wasn't fooling me.

"A while," he said, and I tried to remember the last time he had used his gun. When we had been standing there, my gun aimed at Ryan… I had heard the clicks of his empty gun.

"Just take mine. We'll all be safe if you have the loaded one."

"We'll figure it out later," he said, and I could tell that he wasn't thrilled that I had outed him about his empty gun. Maybe if everyone believed it was loaded, he believed it too. Surely we could just divide up the bullets we had left, but maybe that's what he planned to do later.

What if we ran into HOME? Or the dog-beasts? Without bullets we were in trouble and while I didn't know much about guns, I was pretty sure we couldn't have much ammo left in any of them.

If we wanted any chance to survive all of this and make it to Michigan, not only would we need water and food, but Penn would need ammunition. Well, we all would. And we'd need a lot more than whatever it was we had left.

We drove for ten minutes before I couldn't stand the tension in the air any longer. I could feel Penn's stress permeating the air, and I needed a distraction.

"Hey Dean?" I said in a soft voice.

"Yeah?"

"Would you be so kind as to turn on the radio?" I batted my eyes even though I knew he couldn't see them in the dark car.

"The radio? What for?" he asked, and I didn't know if that mean he hadn't felt the same tension I did or if it just hadn't bothered him.

"I don't know... maybe the whole world hadn't been destroyed. Maybe we can pick up a radio station, listen to some music," I said not believing a single word I'd said.

"Right," Dean said, but he turned on the radio anyway. He clicked the search button, but it just zoomed through the stations, zipping through the numbers until it stopped for a brief second and then continued. It was mostly static, but it was strange that it had stopped. Had there been voices?

"Did you hear that? Go back," I said leaning forward. I was the only one excited. Alice was trying to get rest while Sienna and Carter were silently flirting with one another.

Dean tried to go back, but it kept jumping over the station. All he could do was keep pushing the buttons because there was no dial for him to try to tune it in more accurately. The button only wanted to stop at stations that were coming in clear… which there were none.

"Hmm, there's nothing there," Dean said as he reached over to click the radio off. But something made him push the seek button one more time instead. This time it stopped on the number. The station was coming in and my heart stopped for a second when I heard a voice.

Chapter eleven.

After a few seconds I realized it wasn't a person speaking… well, technically it was, but it was a recording. It was set up to say the same thing over and over again.

When it said the date, August 5th, I looked around to see if anyone else was as shocked as I was. If the date was correct, it had been more than a year since the storms hit. No one seemed overly surprised about the date, they seemed more surprised they were hearing a voice on the radio even if it was just a recording.

It felt weird how I had no sense of time anymore. Of course, the recording could easily just make up a date and I'd be none the wiser. What were the odds that this random man that made the recording actually had been keeping track of the date? Needless to say I was skeptical, but it also didn't seem impossible.

"If you are hearing this, there is a place where survivors are gathering. We want to rebuild. Take back what is ours," the husky voice said emphatically.

"Is this for real?" Sienna asked grabbing Penn's seat and shaking it. She looked as though she was seeing a finish line, but I was skeptical.

"It's probably HOME," I said not turning to look at her. "It's another trick to lead people into their camps."

We listened as the voice continued, "We are located at a U. S. Government Air Force base. There is plenty of food, water, shelter and we even have a small army. It's imperative that you do not trust the other groups out there. We are the real U. S. Military located at a real U. S. Military base. If you are approached by others... run."

Then the recording gave out the location and brief directions before starting over with the same message. They had even given out the longitude and latitude coordinates. It seemed very official, but of course, after everything we'd been through, I didn't trust it.

Penn continued down the highway. He didn't pull over to discuss. I was certain he had the same concerns I did.

"Should we check it out?" Sienna asked glancing at Alice briefly. Alice's head was resting against the back of the seat and her eyes were closed. "I think we should check it out. What if they have a doctor there?"

"We don't need a doctor," Penn said with both hands on the steering wheel. He didn't even bother to slow the car down while we discussed things. "All we need is food water and rest."

"We need those things too, but it wouldn't hurt to have a doctor look at Alice," Sienna said.

"They probably don't have a doctor," Penn said in a low voice.

Dean looked at me and then at Sienna. I wasn't sure what he saw when he looked at her, but he settled his eyes on Penn. "What if we are making a mistake? What if this is real? This could be our only chance to find others like us."

I shook my head. Dean had been through all the same things I had been through, well almost all of them. I didn't know how he could even consider checking it out.

"It's just another trick," I said crossing my arms in front of my chest.

"And what if you're wrong?" Dean said looking back and forth between Penn and I. It was like he thought he had to convince us. Change our minds. It was so dark in the car I didn't think he could see my expression, but I was worried going would be a mistake.

"What if you're wrong?" I countered.

"I'm not saying you're right or wrong, what I'm saying is we should check it out. They are on the radio… it could easily be the real deal. The military could have been prepared for something like this. What if this is it?" Dean said, his eyes twinkling with the aqua color from the dashboard lights.

There was a small part of me that worried about the miniscule chance that I was wrong. That we might be driving away from safety and security. Food and water. But a bigger part of me, the one that had struggled with HOME and the resistance, was far too afraid to find out if I was right or wrong.

"There!" Sienna said pointing to a sign that indicated the way to the U. S. Military base. "Look how close we are! Let's just check it out."

I guessed that's why the station had come in better, it was because we were closer. Why was their broadcasting signal so small?

Penn shook his head so hard I worried he was going to hurt his neck. "No way. Especially not at night. Are you crazy?"

"Well then we find somewhere to park and wait until morning," Dean said using a tone that made it sound as though he wasn't asking, rather he was telling. It wasn't often he'd say what we should do, but this time he was and he wanted Penn and I to make our peace with it. "I think we need to check. We'll be careful and if anything looks off, we'll turn around."

"We're almost out of ammo. It's a bad idea," I said stomping my foot on the floor.

"Penn can sort it out. I'm sure we can divide up the bullets. We can't miss this chance... this could be the real thing. They know about the other camps, and not only that, but they warned against going to them. That has to count for something," Dean said throwing his hand into the air. He felt as strongly about checking it out as I did about not checking it out.

It wasn't like we could separate. I wouldn't let them out of my sight. There was no way I wanted things going back to like they had been when I was alone in Alaska.

We were struggling to find water and the only food we had were snacks. And with our lack of ammo it was risky to travel the roads. Things were definitely bleak, but was this the answer?

We'd found shelter, food and water before, we could do it again. Food supplies were extremely low, but I was sure there were untapped food sources somewhere out there, we just had to think outside the box like Alice had with her hotel suggestion.

"Are there any resistance camps you know of around here" Penn said, and I knew he was directing his question at Carter.

"Not that I know of," Carter answered, but I saw his shoulders move up and down out of the corner of my eye. He wasn't sure. He didn't have any idea about any other resistance camp, he'd only known about the one he'd been in, or so I assumed.

Whoever it was could easily be the resistance, but the warning to avoid the other camps was odd. Unless there were even more groups of people out there that we needed to avoid.

"If it's HOME... they'll probably kill me on sight, you know that right?" Penn said turning his head slightly towards Dean before he returned his gaze back to the road.

Dean looked down and then over his shoulder at Sienna before he twisted around to look at me, "If it's HOME, they'll probably kill us all. That's why we have to be careful."

If there had been any HOME camps or bases down this way and Penn had known about them, there would be no way he'd even consider checking it out. But I could tell by the way he was looking around the area as he slowed the car, that he was going to do it, if only to satisfy Dean's curiosity.

Penn had been out of touch with HOME for a long time. For all he knew there were HOME camps and spies strategically scattered everywhere.

This could be one of those places and he just wasn't aware.

"I don't know about this," I said feeling my stomach twist into a tight knot, or maybe it was trying to eat itself again. I never felt hunger pangs any more, instead it felt more like little critters were gnawing at my insides. They usually went away if I ignored them. But of course, it would always come back later to remind me when I needed to eat, whether or not food was available.

"OK," Penn said after several minutes of silence. "I'll head out and check the place in the morning when I can see better."

"You're not going alone," I said leaning forward.

"We all go in the morning," Dean said taking charge. It was the first time since Owen's death he'd stepped up and made a decision about what we were going to do. If Penn and I shut him down now, I didn't know exactly how he'd take it.

For some reason he wanted to check out this place. Maybe he was having visions of a safe place with tons of food and water, and he didn't want to be wrong about it. Why continue struggling if there was a place we could go? Maybe we'd be stuck in Michigan worried about where the next meal would come from, always thinking about when HOME or the resistance would come and attack us. Why go through all that if we could just stop here and never have to worry again?

"Ugh! OK, fine. We'll go in the morning. I'll find a side road for now. We'll eat something, and take turns getting rest so we are alert as possible," Penn said as if he was trying to take charge of the situation. After all, Penn had been leading ever since we lost Owen. It hadn't been a role he asked for, it was one that sort of just fell into his lap. And he'd done a fine job.

"Right," Dean said as he sat up and straightened his spine.

Ten minutes or so down the road, Penn pulled over into the ditch and parked the car. He twisted sideways in his seat, "Give me your guns."

Dean and I passed over our guns and we all watched as Penn rearranged the ammo between the guns. He checked them over and then handed them back.

"I'll get some snacks out," Dean said as he gripped his gun handle and opened the passenger door. Besides the lights from the car we were in complete darkness.

I was almost one hundred percent positive there wouldn't be anyone wandering around in the dark. They wouldn't be able to see anything, well, except for the lights from our car. But they probably couldn't make it this far unless they were carrying their own light and then we'd spot them coming from a mile away. It wasn't likely someone would just be walking around aimlessly and happen upon our car, but Dean was ready with his gun just in case.

We feasted on our snacks, probably more than we should have eaten considering it was our only food supply and it was limited. Then we took turns sleeping so that when morning rolled around, we'd be ready to make our way to the military base and check out the possibility of finally finding help.

* * *

The sun was barely over the horizon when Dean started waking us all up. I couldn't quite figure it out, but Dean clearly didn't have the same reservations about the military base that Penn and I had. Perhaps it was just desperation. Desperate for help. Desperate for a break.

After we each had another snack, we were out on the road heading back towards the sign that indicated where the military base was located. My palms were sweating so badly I had to wipe them on my pants. And even though I'd eaten, it still felt as though my stomach was chewing on itself.

When we saw the base come into view, Penn parked the car. He tried to hide it from view by parking behind some dead shrubbery, but his plan hadn't really worked. The car was still visible from most angles. Anyone paying the least bit of attention to their surroundings would see it. But they probably wouldn't be able to start it unless they knew which wires to touch together.

"Dean, Ros, walk with me in front," Penn said gesturing for me to stand on his left and Dean on his right side. We formed sort of a triangle with Sienna, Carter and Alice tucked in behind us.

As we got closer to the gate, I noticed the tall chain-link fence that surrounded the entire base. For the most part it looked intact, but I did question the amount of security it would provide.

Maybe everyone inside kept to a particular building or area, but since I didn't see anyone moving around, I wondered how many survivors were even inside. People weren't milling about working on things like I'd imagine a place trying to rebuild would be like.

It was possible that something had happened and everyone was gone. Although, the recording had mentioned the date. I wished we would have listened to the recording again, maybe it always said the same date. And if the date changed, then we'd know there were people still inside.

Some of the buildings looked to have been torn down. There were piles of wood, brick and concrete blocks in heaps where buildings had once stood. But there were plenty of buildings still standing, and several of them looked very sturdy and secure. Perhaps if there was still anyone here, those were the ones they used.

"Where is everyone?" Sienna whispered looking out between Penn and my shoulders.

"I don't know... it's awfully quiet," Penn said and I could tell he was considering turning back. And I would have agreed.

"Step forward and lower your weapons," someone shouted from above.

"Not in a million years," Penn said gripping the handle of his gun tighter. We needed to retreat, and based on the look on Penn's face, he knew it too.

The harsh voice laughed. It sounded similar to the voice we had heard on the recording.

"Come on now, we can't have you shooting up the place. I need to keep my people safe." He let out a loose cough. "I get it though... you don't trust us. Why should you? My guess is that you've seen some bad shit out there, but kid, we are the U. S. Military and we're here to help," he said as if words would somehow ease our concerns. If he knew at all what it had been like out there, he would have understood why we weren't lowering our guns. He would have also known words were just that... words.

"If it's all the same," Penn said tilting his head towards his gun.

"It's not," the man said as the gate behind us closed. The loud clanging noise startled me and I took a step away. Wires sprouted up out of the dirt and tripped me. I tried to get my balance, but I was too twisted up in whatever it was around my feet and ankles, and I fell to the ground.

Penn came towards me to help me, but he got caught up in the wires too. He hit the ground hard but kept his gun at the ready the whole time he fell.

"The rest of you need to GET DOWN!" the voice shouted, and two men came around the corner. One of the two men was carrying a large gun. I didn't know what kind of gun it was, but I knew it could probably take all of us out if the man holding it wanted to. The one that had been doing all the talking pointed his gun at Penn, "Now drop your guns."

I placed mine on the ground about an inch away from me. Penn did the same. I couldn't see

Dean but I'm sure he put his down as well.

"Kick it here," the guy with the gun pointed at Penn said but he was talking to Dean. I heard Dean sigh and then kick it towards the man.

The second guy walked over with his gun pointed at me and quickly picked up my gun and tucked it into his pants. Then he picked up Penn's gun and held on to it as he walked back towards the one that was doing all the talking.

"Now, is that all of your weapons?" the man asked. He must have been able to tell by the looks on our faces that we'd given them everything, "Good. Now no funny business, ya hear?"

Penn stared at the man that was holding the gun that was pointed at him. I knew Penn didn't need a gun. If given an opportunity, he could easily take out the two armed men, but how many others were here? Were there other guns we couldn't see pointed at us too?

Dean looked at me, and I could tell by the look on his face that he was blaming himself. He had made the wrong choice about this place. And we had walked right into their trap. They'd probably heard or seen us coming down the road… they'd been prepared.

"Welcome to the U. S. Military base! I'm Cy and this is Sargent Bobby Lee. Now, get the fuck up off of the ground and stand at attention," Cy said as he tapped his gun to remind us who was in charge. Bobby Lee walked over and cut the wires around our feet so we could stand. "And like I said, don't even think about trying anything stupid. See those towers? Snipers."

I looked at Penn and saw him squinting at the nearest tower. He shook his head ever so slightly from side-to-side which made me think he hadn't seen anyone up in the towers.

"Eyes front and center!" Cy shouted only inches from my face.

I leaned back, "Sorry." I tried not to react to the smell of his dreadful breath. It smelled as though he'd been eating raw roadkill. I laced my fingers together behind my back and straightened my back.

"Shut up! Walk," Cy said, pointing with his gun. Carter and Sienna were to my left, and Carter didn't hesitate to lead the way. He marched, waiting for someone to tell him to stop.

Cy was at the back of the line and his friend, Sargent Bobby Lee was walking off to the side of our line. He kept his gun up in case he needed to use it, his eyes shifting from one of us to the next. It didn't seem at all like this was the first time they had done this.

"Halt!" Cy shouted and Carter stopped so abruptly he almost fell.

Bobby Lee stepped forward and opened the door to the small shed we were facing. He stepped back and gestured with the barrel of his gun for us to step inside.

"Aw come on!" I said throwing my hands into the air. I could feel Penn's eyes staring at the back of my head.

Bobby Lee looked at me and then shifted his eyes back to Cy. I looked over my shoulder, worried about what Cy would do about me talking without having been talked to first. But I was lucky. He didn't do anything. He just smirked and nodded at the shed.

"Inside… now," Bobby Lee ordered, tapping me on the shoulder with his gun when I didn't move. I moved my feet and followed Sienna inside the shed. Once we were all inside they didn't say anything, they just closed the door and locked us inside.

Chapter twelve.

The shed had been completely cleared out. There wasn't a single sign left to indicate what the storage shed had been used for before its current purpose of storing people. Penn pushed on the wall, it had a small amount of give, but overall it was sturdy. We wouldn't be able to kick through it or knock it down.

Carter, Sienna, and Alice sat down on the floor while Penn moved around the room feeling every inch of the walls from top to bottom. He was probably trying to look for some kind of weak spot, but I didn't think he was finding anything. I paced back and forth in the small space, while Dean banged his head lightly against the wall.

"What's the plan?" Sienna said, and I could tell she was trying to play it cool around Carter. If he hadn't been here, I was pretty sure she would have been far more upset about our current situation.

"I don't have one," Penn said, slamming his fist into the side wall.

"It's hard to accept at first, but they do feed us," a soft voice said. It sounded as though it was coming from the other side of the wall Penn had just hit. "Well, sometimes they feed us. I mean, it's not like three square meals a day, but enough to keep us alive. Square meals... what does that saying mean? Meals aren't really square, except sandwiches, they are kind of square."

Penn looked at me and then at the wall, "What is this place? Are we in some kind of holding cell?"

"You know, I've wondered the same thing," the soft male voice on the other side of the wall said. "But I've been in here fore a while now."

"Are you alone?" Penn asked pressing his ear to the wall.

"Well I am right now," the man said with a panicked chuckle. "But I came here looking for help. And as you may have already figured out, there isn't any help here."

Penn gestured for me to stand next to him and then pointed towards my ear, and then soundlessly tapped the wall. He wanted me to listen too. But I couldn't hear anything. I assumed the person talking to us on the other side was sitting still, and it did seem as though they were probably alone.

"How many did you come here with? Where are they now?" Penn asked staring into my eyes as he waited for the answer. I looked back, as if his eyes would provide me some kind of magical insight into what was going on.

"Just my sister and her boyfriend, but they are gone now. They took them. One at a time and now it's just me. You should have heard my sister wail when they pulled her boyfriend away. It was traumatic."

I frowned at Penn. Would that be what happened to us? They'd tear us away from one another.

"How long ago did they take them?" Penn asked, his words melted into one another as if he couldn't ask the questions fast enough.

"My sister maybe three weeks ago, and her boyfriend was about two weeks before that? I'm not sure… I'm having a hard time keeping track of time in here. And now I've been alone for so long. Each day has started to bleed into the next," he said with a thick sniff. "Sorry I know I'm not much help. Sucks you're in here too, but I am glad I have neighbors."

"Right," Penn said pulling his ear away from the wall. He turned away and whispered, "I think he's alone and I think he's telling the truth."

I nodding in agreement. Why would the men take them one by one and weeks apart? I didn't know what was going on in this place but I didn't have a good feeling about it. Maybe they just didn't trust us in groups, but then why did they wait so long between?

"Where are you guys from?" our neighbor asked. Penn's eyes were wide. "How many of you are there in there? It sounded like a lot!"

I knew he didn't want to answer the guy, but I didn't know if it would really matter either. There was always a chance we were wrong, and the guy wasn't telling the truth. He could have been planted in there to gather information about us.

What if our neighbor was a spy? Penn had to be careful what he said to the man. In fact, maybe it would have been better not to have talked to him at all.

We hadn't learned anything from him about the camp. Maybe it was because he didn't know anything about this place, or maybe he was intentionally keeping things from us. All I knew was that we couldn't trust him.

"Just a few of us in here," Penn answered rubbing his hands together. I could tell our neighbor was making him nervous, and I'm sure the situation we were stuck in didn't help matters.

"OK… well hello to your friends," he said with a small nervous chuckle.

Penn held up his hand and shook his head. He didn't want any of us to answer. They already knew how many of us were in the shed, but I think Penn was afraid that our neighbor would only try to engage more if we all started talking.

Our neighbor asked a few more brief questions and Penn answered them with as few words as possible. He must have picked up on the fact that Penn didn't want to talk, because he stopped asking him questions. For all we knew, the guy was just lonely and looking for someone to talk to. Just a way to pass the time.

I couldn't help but wonder what had happened to his friends once they had been taken. If what he said was true, would they start taking us out of the shed one by one? If I was left in here alone after the men out there took everyone from me, I wouldn't be trying to strike up conversations, I'd be sitting in here crying and freaking out.

"We have to get out of here," I whispered and shook the door. I didn't know what they had used to lock us inside, but it seemed secure.

"It's no use," our neighbor said loudly so we could hear him over the rattling door. "We tried everything too."

I looked at Dean and then at Penn but he just shook his head. It wasn't like I was going to say anything anyway.

Dean kept his head down most of the time. I let my body slide down the wall until I was sitting on the ground, my shoulder lightly resting against Dean's. He held his body stiff. It was like he hadn't even noticed that I was next to him.

I wanted to tell him that I didn't blame him for any of this, but he wouldn't have listened to me anyway. He knew it was his idea to come. He had practically demanded it, but he had only been doing what he thought was best. The last person he probably wanted to hear any of that from was me since I had voiced my opinion against the whole idea.

This wasn't his fault. It wasn't like any of us knew what would happen if we came. Of course I wished it would have been the safe haven it claimed to be, but it didn't seem to be. Maybe something worse would have happened to us if we had kept going on the road today. There was no point in wondering about the what-ifs... we needed to deal with the what-nows and get ourselves out of here.

I opened my mouth to tell him we'd get out of here, but I closed it when I heard the loud clanging noise against the shed walls. They were outside, pounding and being rough with something. When our shed door didn't open, I knew they were at our neighbor's door.

"Oww! God! So unnecessary!" our neighbor squawked. He tried to hide it but his voice was filled with fear. "I'm going with you. It's not like you have to be so rough!"

It sounded like the men were pulling him along with them. Our neighbor said he was going willingly, but it didn't sound that way. I couldn't help but wonder if they were being extra rough for our benefit.

"What are you going to do to me?" he said, his voice trailing off as he was moved further and further away. Then I didn't hear the sound of movement anymore. There was nothing. Just complete silence.

"Jesus Christ," Penn said softly into the silence. The words almost seemed to hang in the air. If someone walked by later, they'd still hear them. "We need to get out of this place."

Penn stood up looking more panicked than I'd ever seen him. He started shaking and kicking the door. He faced the door, balled up his fists and growled at the door before giving it one final kick as hard as he could. But the door just rattled back and forth.

I glanced around and everyone was staring at him. Even Dean looked up. Carter and Alice almost looked scared by the outburst.

I walked over to him and put my hand on his shoulder. He aggressively shrugged me off and Dean took notice. I held my palm up signaling that I was fine and that I could handle Penn.

He shook his head and turned to look at me.

His eyes were filled with anguish and I knew he was sorry for how he'd reacted to my touch. Penn didn't actually say the words, but I could tell he felt bad.

"We'll come up with a plan. Just stop for a moment and think," I said taking a small careful step towards him.

"I can't any more!" Penn shouted as he put his arm up against the wall and drove his head into the back of his arm. "I'm just so sick of all this. I'm so tired."

Penn had been our caretaker since the minute he wanted to step up and prove that he was on our side. He'd been working overtime at keep us all safe. I didn't blame him for being exhausted, but I didn't know what to say to fix things either.

It was like HOME had control over his brain. He had been conditioned to be a super fighter but now, after all this time of having his switch flipped in the on position, he needed it off for awhile. It was draining the life out of him. I hated watching as he searched around inside of himself for the off switch.

What if after everything HOME had done to him there wasn't an off switch? Maybe that's what he was worried about. I wanted to tell him that once we got somewhere he could feel safe, he'd be better, but I didn't know if that was true. Maybe we wouldn't ever find anywhere safe enough or maybe he wouldn't be able to turn himself off.

"OK," Penn said taking deep breaths. He bent over like he was playing short-stop for a baseball team as he reeled himself back in. "I'm going to sit down now."

"That's probably a good idea," I said with as gentle of a smile as I could manage. He didn't look at me to notice it anyway.

I started to pace back and forth in front of the door. Every so often I would think I heard something moving around outside, but when I put my ear to the wall, I couldn't hear anything.

The hours passed by, but since I couldn't see outside I had no idea what time of day it was. Carter had his arm around Sienna and she was resting her head on his shoulder. I couldn't tell but it seemed as though they were both asleep. Or as close to it as anyone could get.

Dean grabbed his wrist hard and rubbed it, keeping his eyes focused on the twisting movements. Alice was curled up on the ground with her back to me. Her body slowly moved up and down as if she was asleep. With how sick she was, she needed as much rest as she could get.

Penn's head would tilt to the side every so often as he started to drift off, but something would startle him awake. He'd look around quickly, remember where he was and then rest his head back against the wall until the same thing happened again.

I didn't feel tired, although I'm sure I was. My veins were surging with the desire to escape and the adrenaline pumping through my body gave no indication of letting up. I kept moving around the room trying to burn off some of the energy.

Even when everyone was asleep, I was still up walking around the box we were trapped inside.

It reminded me of when we were stuck in the underground shelter and I just wanted to move my body. It felt more like a need. I had done various exercises… like the jumping jacks I'd done with Ryan.

The feeling was the same. I had to move. And I was about to start doing jumping jacks when I heard the *clink-clank* noises outside of our shed.

Chapter thirteen.

Penn's eyes popped wide open. He had heard the noises outside the shed. His body was absolutely still. It was like he went from being completely asleep to fully awake in less than a full second. He stared at the door, looking like he was ready to launch himself at it.

I turned and kept my focus on the door too. The dryness of the air stung my eyes since I refused to blink. If I looked away from the door for even a second, I might miss whatever was about to happen and that could mean life or death.

Whoever was outside of the shed wasn't saying anything. There were noises of something being moved around and then I heard rattling at the door. It sounded as if they were undoing the locks.

I stepped back. Everyone looked scared, except for Penn who looked neutral. I'd seen the look before and I knew he was getting ready to act, should he need to.

I wanted to be ready to help him, but I was clueless on how to flip my switch into the on position. I probably didn't have one. All I could do was wait and watch.

Dean was on the floor somewhere behind me against the wall. I was about to nudge him with my foot when something reached out and grabbed around my ankle. It took a second, but I realized quickly that it was Dean, and thankfully I had been able to stop the scream that had almost escaped.

He stood up silently and stepped out in front of me. We watched the door as it was pulled open. I expected someone to step inside, but what entered the small shed was the barrel of a rifle.

"Up against the wall," a deep voice said. It sounded as if whoever was speaking was trying to disguise their real voice. Or maybe sound tougher than they actually were. Maybe both.

The gun bobbed and pointed at each one of us in turn as I stepped back and pressed my back into the wall. If I could have backed through the wall, I would have.

When I tried to see the person behind the door, I noticed that it was dark outside. It was night, but I didn't know what time of night it was. All I could say for sure was that it was too dark to see anyone clearly.

"Put your hands where I can see them," the voice said in a false low octave.

My body reflexively jumped as a plastic tray slid across the ground and into the middle of the room. Before I looked back up at the gun, I noticed there were bottles of water on the tray. I wanted to dive for one of them and thank the gun for bringing us the lifesaving liquid, but I didn't.

The barrel of the gun slowly disappeared from the room and then the door slammed shut. Penn leapt towards the door, but whoever had been on the other side was prepared. They had the locks back in place in record time. It was as if they'd expected that reaction.

"If you are going to do stupid things like that, and we can't trust you, maybe we won't bring you food any more. If you aren't going to be good little boys and girls, I won't be opening this door again and you can bet your short little lives on that one," the voice said. This time I recognized the voice. It was the same one from earlier today, the one that had said his name was Cy. The one that I presumed was in charge of this place. Whatever it was.

Penn slammed his fist into the door once and hard. The door rattled and shivered to a stop. I knew what word he wanted to shout out at our captors based solely on how he had hit the door. But he didn't yell it… although I imagined he was saying it repeatedly in his head. He probably wanted to tell Cy everything he thought of him, but maybe he decided against it because he didn't want to get anyone killed. They had the guns. For now, they had the power.

I waited until I didn't hear the movement outside any longer before opening my mouth to speak. "What did they bring? We can't drink that water can we?"

"Why not?" Sienna said, her voice was thick with saliva. The desire for water was apparent even in how she spoke. She looked at the tray but she didn't move towards it. None of us did. We all thought it was some kind of trick, maybe a bomb or some kind of booby trap. No one wanted to find out what would happen if we touched it.

"Maybe it's unsafe… contaminated or something. Or maybe it's poisoned," I said crossing my arms in front of my chest. There was probably nothing I could do or say that would stop any of them, myself included, from drinking the water. No matter how paranoid I was about it, I had no doubt that I would soon gladly be drinking down my entire portion.

"Why would they bother poisoning us? They have guns. If they wanted us dead, they could have killed us by now. Instead they are feeding us," Penn said with a shrug as he crouched down and examined the things on the tray. He poked at the water bottles as though he thought they might decide to just walk off of the tray.

He was right. The water was probably fine, as was whatever else was on the tray.

"Not much there," Carter said as he slowly moved forward to have a look at the other things on the tray. Sienna held onto his shirt and followed along as they inched closer.

There were two paper bowls filled with questionable looking baked beans, and another bowl filled with what I hoped was an open can of uncooked clam chowder. There were random chunks sitting in the gelatinous soup that maybe were potatoes.

But what we were all most interested in were the six plastic bottles filled with water. It looked so pure and clean it practically sparkled in the poorly lit shed.

The three metal spoons on the tray were the complete opposite of the water of life. They looked as though they hadn't been cleaned after the last time they had been used. It appeared they were coated in dried ketchup.

"A bottle of water for each of us... they must have a supply nearby," Penn said, looking at the bowls of food. Half a bowl of food wouldn't be nearly enough but it was better than nothing at all. "So who's going to eat the white, lumpy one?"

I was pretty sure everyone was thinking the same thing I was, that it looked like regurgitated food. It made the baked beans look like fillet mignon.

Dean stepped forward scrunching his eyebrows together. He was volunteering to take half the chunky soup, or so it seemed.

Penn raised his eyebrow and pushed the bowl of white slop towards him, "You want the white crap?"

"I'll take half... it's food isn't it?" Dean said reaching out his hand to accept the bowl. A look of regret washed over his face as he sloshed the soup and watched the chunks move around heavily.

"I think that's up for debate," Penn said curling up one side of his mouth. He put his hand on his stomach and turned away from the bowl of thick white goop.

Dean pinched the paper bowl slightly so he could pour the soup into his mouth. He stopped every so often to chew the chunks I had originally thought were potatoes, but now I wasn't so sure. He looked at Penn and rubbed his belly, "Mmm, mmm!"

"OK... any volunteers for the second half of the white stuff?" Penn asked, and I figured I might as well take one for the team because of the whole

Dean and I being a couple thing. I should support him, but I was surprised when I didn't have to. I didn't even get a chance to volunteer.

Alice stepped up next to Dean. She tilted her head slightly to the side and put her hand on her hip. She smiled at Dean and I couldn't help but feel somewhat annoyed.

"I'll take it. I don't mind... I'm sure I've had much, much worse," she said pulling her hair back and twisting it around her left shoulder. I shook my head and narrowed my eyes. Was she showing some kind of interest in Dean? If she was, it wasn't going to work and she sure wouldn't be winning any favors with me. Then again, maybe she was just trying to make things easier for everyone.

I let out a puff of air that blew a strand of hair out of my face. "Well then, I guess that's settled."

I watched to make sure Dean completely finished his portion before handing her the bowl. I didn't want her contaminating the bowl with her germs and increasing his chances of catching whatever it was she had. Although, we were all so close together most of the time that we were all likely to catch it anyway.

I didn't have to worry about it because she stood next to him patiently waiting for her half with a big, dumb smile on her face. She looked at him, blinking her eyes while she waited, but the only part I really cared about was that she waited.

Once he finished, he handed her the bowl and smiled back at her. He picked up one of the bottles at random and chugged it down. Then he stepped away from the group and sat back down leaning his back against the wall. He looked unhappy, frustrated and as though he was trying to devise a plan to get us out of here.

Penn and I shared one of the bowls of baked beans. We didn't bother with the dirty spoons either, surely using those disgusting things would have gotten us sick too. A different kind of sick, maybe, but definitely sick. Penn bent the bowl in the same way he'd seen Dean do it and ate his portion.

After I finished mine, I grabbed a bottle of water and drank it down. At first I was going to save it… make it last because I didn't know when I'd get water again, but I couldn't help myself. I drank it far too fast and even though it helped my stomach feel full, I thought that maybe I was going to get a stomach ache.

I sat down next to Dean with my hands on my slightly puffed out belly as I watched the others drink from the water bottles in much the same way as Dean and I had done. Fast. They all had the same look on their face. Eyes closed with a small smile, not wanting to reach the bottom of the bottle.

Dean and I were against one wall, Carter, Sienna and Alice were to our left and Penn was straight across from me. We didn't really look at one another. Everyone was quiet as we stared at the door as if waiting for something to happen.

Penn reached forward and pocketed the dirty spoons. Then he collected all the empty water bottles and lined them up next to him on the side furthest from the door. I was pretty sure the guys holding us would take them away first chance they got. They probably reused the bottles the same as they had the spoons. Penn could probably use the tray for a weapon, and it would surprise me if someone hadn't already tried that.

I didn't know if he had a plan in mind for his collection or if he was just hoarding them in case he came up with an idea. He started tracing around the pattern stamped on the tray and I watched as his finger lazily moved around the indents and grooves. It slowed down each time he started the pattern over.

I looked up and saw his eyes as they were slowly closing. He fought to keep them open, but he was losing the battle. I was happy he was getting some rest, even if it seemed to be odd timing. Then again, we were all tired, maybe a mildly full belly helped him get some shut-eye. But it didn't matter… if anything happened he'd be instantly awake to try to save the day. It was just how his brain worked.

When I looked over and saw Sienna sleeping on Carter's chest and his head tilted sharply to the side, it surprised me how quickly everyone had fallen asleep. Alice, too, was laying on the ground next to Carter's legs with her eyes closed and her body gently rising and falling with each breath.

"Isn't that weird?" I said nudging my elbow into Dean's side. He didn't answer. There was a soft rustling noise as his body tipped to the side, and he fell awkwardly into the corner of the room.

"You too?"

I scooted forward to look at him. He looked scrunched up and uncomfortable in the corner but I wasn't sure I'd be able to adjust him myself. His neck was cranked towards the side so far that I could see the muscles and tendons in his neck stretching to their limits.

I tried to pull him back into a more comfortable position but either he was too heavy or I was so weak that I couldn't move him myself. He was out cold. I couldn't even remember that last time any of us had slept that deeply.

My heart jumped for a second. I was worried that maybe something had happened, but he was still breathing. He was taking shallow, sleepy breaths that moved over his chest like a gentle wave.

"Dean," I whispered as I shook him. I felt a little scared being the only one awake. "Wake up!"

He didn't wake up. He didn't even come close to waking up. I shook him harder, but it didn't make any difference.

I scurried across the floor like a frightened critter towards Penn. My fingers gripped his arms tightly, and I shook him aggressively. He didn't wake up either.

"Oh, no. No, no, no, no, no," I whispered shaking Penn even harder. He started slumping down towards the ground. I couldn't stop him from sliding, all I could do was try to make his movement a touch gentler.

I buried my face into my hands at the same time I heard someone at the door. It sounded like they were we going to come inside. I quickly looked over my shoulder at the door like a wild animal and I did the first thing that popped into my head.

I played dead.

Chapter fourteen.

I didn't look up, move or breathe when I heard the door open. There were at least two people inside the shed. They didn't talk, but I was sure I had heard the scuffles of more than one pair of feet.

"What the shit?" one of the voices said in a hushed, deep voice. Bobby Lee. "Did we screw it up again?"

"Did *you* screw it up again," a second voice, Cy, said. It seemed as though they were trying to disguise them, but I was getting better at picking out their voices.

I wondered what they'd do if they didn't find what they were looking for, which I assumed was me because I was the only one that hadn't fallen asleep. Would they start killing us? But that wouldn't make much sense. They could have done that without drugging us.

"Oh shit man, I bet they shared again," Bobby Lee groaned.

"Don't think so. Then we'd probably have two awake instead of all asleep. Hmm," Cy said as I heard the movement of feet.

"This one's out cold," Bobby Lee said in a dopey voice. He'd given up on trying to disguise it. Why would they need to disguise their voices anyway? And why were their two voices the only ones I'd heard? Where was everyone else? I guess, for whatever reason, Cy and Bobby Lee did all the dirty work.

"This one too," Cy grunted.

"Come out, come out wherever you are!" Bobby Lee said in a voice that chilled my bones.

I didn't need to open my eyes to see they were moving their way towards me. Somehow I managed to keep myself calm and unmoving, even when they poked me with what I assumed was the same rifle I had seen when they brought the food into the shed.

"This doesn't make sense," Bobby Lee said as he kicked the dirt. I was pelted in the back of my head with several little pebbles.

"Let's just shoot them. One by one. Start with the one by the door," Cy said and I could imagine him grinning as he looked around.

I could feel my heart rate increase, and I was having trouble controlling my breathing. When one of them grabbed me by the arm that had the bandage on it, I knew they had noticed my body movements. I managed not to scream out in pain even though it felt like bee stings on my arm where he touched the burned skin.

My eyes popped open, and I saw Bobby Lee standing by the door. His gun at his side. He didn't have any intention of shooting any of us. I wanted to slap the ear-to-ear smile off of his chunky face with a piece of steel wool.

"Clever little girl aren't you?" Cy said, nodding as though he appreciated my attempt. But not enough to let me go.

Cy dragged me out of the shed as I kicked

and struggled against him. I shouted for Dean and then for Penn, but they didn't budge.

Bobby Lee slammed the door shut, and they were out of my sight. I managed to get my arm free, and I crawled across the ground towards the fence even though I saw it was closed.

"Help me with her," Cy said trying to grab my arm again, and all I could do was swat and kick at him to keep him away.

Bobby Lee haphazardly put the lock in place, keeping his eyes mostly on me. The look on his face was a creepy, slimy grin that made my stomach hurt. It was like he enjoyed watching me fight even though there was no hope for me.

"Did you lock it tight this time?" Cy growled as he reached for my leg. I kicked at his hand with the other leg.

"Of course I did. Go check it if you want," Bobby Lee said as if he was offended by the question. But a look flashed across his face that I knew meant he had screwed up once before. He almost looked as though he wanted to double check the door but he nodded repeatedly as if he was confident and capable. To me, he just looked like a big, dumb cartoon character.

"Get her leg," Cy instructed, and I tried to kick at them both. Once Cy got one leg, Bobby Lee was able to get the other.

I reached forward and tried to scratch Bobby Lee in the face, but missed. He caught my arm, and I was forced to give up. At least for now.

"Where are you taking me?" I asked looking around the camp. Were the snipers pointing their guns at me? Were others on their way to help them? I shifted my eyes around the camp as best as I could, trying to memorize everything I was seeing. If I got free, I wanted to know which way would lead me back to my friends and which way was out of the camp.

I listened, but I didn't hear anyone else around. The whole place was so quiet it was eerie.

All of the buildings around us had locks on the outside of the doors. In most cases, there were multiple padlocks in place, I guessed for extra security. Maybe our neighbor would pop out at any second and confirm that he was, in fact, placed there to try to learn more about us.

"Shut up," Cy said, his voice originating from his chest and rumbling out of his nose and mouth.

I looked over my shoulder and took a mental photograph of the shed my friends were in.

The shed was close to the front gate and as long as they didn't take me too far away with a lot of twists and turns, I was positive I could make my way back to them. Every time I blinked it was like taking a new photograph that I hoped I could recall if need be.

They dragged me about three buildings away, taking only one turn to the right. If I had to get out of their building, all I had to remember was to take a left turn and then I could check one of the mental pictures in my head. I would be back with my friends in no time. All I had to do was break free from Cy and his dumb lackey and get back to my friends who needed me. Although I had no idea how I'd wake them up and get us out of here.

Bobby Lee opened the door to a larger building. This door didn't have a lock on the outside.

Cy shoved me inside and I tripped over my own feet and fell to the floor. I tried to get myself back onto my feet, but Bobby Lee had his thick sausage-fingers wrapped around my wrist before I could even turn myself around. His dirty fingernails dug into my flesh as he dragged me towards the back wall.

He held my hand up as though he'd done this a hundred times. I felt the cold metal against my wrist. It made a *thunk* when he locked it into place.

Bobby Lee had shackled me to the wall. I swiped my free hand towards his face, aiming for his eyes. My aim was slightly off, but I'd made contact. I scratched his face, and I watched as the blood beaded up in a line across his cheek. I couldn't help but smile.

"Uh! You stupid bitch!" he said and slapped me across the face. It stung, but I didn't want to let it show. He hadn't bothered to take it easy on me either.

I gritted my teeth and stared directly into his angry, hateful gray eyes. If I had been a bit braver, or maybe dumber, I would have spit in his stupid face. But I was almost certain that would lead me down a short path to a painful death. For all I knew I was already on that path.

If he was OK with hitting me, who knew what else he would do if provoked. My goal was to stay alive as long as possible and maybe get myself out of this so I could save my friends.

Bobby Lee gripped my free wrist and held it so tightly my fingers felt numb. He closed the shackle around that wrist. That's when I saw the blood stains and blood splatter on the wall and ground all around me. I wanted to cry. How much time did I have left?

Against the wall, about four feet away from me, was a wood burning stove. The fire inside glowed and crackled. It seemed as though it was laughing at me. It knew what was going to happen, it's seen it before. The fire was telling me that I was being punished for what I had done to Ryan. It was time to pay the price.

Next to the stove was a counter on which a knife was stabbed into the center of a stained cutting board. There was a small table on the other side of the room, near the door, which was holding a pile of guns. Our guns. Plus, maybe, the one Bobby Lee had been holding when they'd come for me and dragged me here.

I was sure that whatever it was they were going to do to me wouldn't involve the guns. I'd probably be begging them to use a gun at some point.

There was only one thing in the room that seemed clean. A polished, pristine table in the center of the room, which looked completely out of place. I assumed they'd taken it from some upscale place and brought it back here. The candle placed in the center of the table made it look like a sacred location even though it was surrounded by ketchup, mustard and barbecue sauce bottles.

This was where the two men lived. It was their living quarters, their dining room, their kitchen and their slaughterhouse all in one. I wasn't sure what was worse, this room or HOME.

Bobby Lee looked at me and shook his head as if he was disappointed. He was mumbling something to Cy that I couldn't hear, and it looked as though Cy was mostly ignoring him.

"Just let me go," I begged as I looked around the room frantically. I was trying to find something that could save me. But when I spotted the long thick bones sticking out of the trash can, I started to shake. The tears rolled down my cheeks and there was nothing I could do to stop them. I was pretty sure I was looking at human bones.

I shook my arms wildly and then stretched the chains out as far as they would go. The rusty metal dug into my wrists. I could feel them making little tears into my flesh as I moved too quickly against the rough, jagged edges.

I kicked and thrust myself forward. If I moved fast enough, perhaps I could pull the chains out of the wall, or break the old shackles, but nothing worked. I tried again, but the only thing that happened was when the chains hit their limit they yanked me back into the wall. The chains and the wall were far stronger than I was.

"No, please no," I said looking at Cy who hungrily smiled at me. "Please! Just let me go!"

The tears flowed faster. There was no way to hold them back. I could feel them, warm against my skin, cutting through the dirt and grime on my face. It made the skin on my cheeks feel tight.

I took several deep breaths and then stared at my feet. It felt as though every ounce of hope and strength I'd ever had was draining out of my body down onto their scummy tiled floor. My slumped, defeated body felt twice as heavy as it should have.

"What are you going to do to me?" I said, even though I was pretty sure I had a good guess what they were going to do. The bones in the trash... the fire roaring... the now dried blood that had been splattered in the same spot I now stood in... it seemed clear. And after it happened to me, it would probably happen to my friends, one by one, in much the same way.

"You are probably aware," Cy said, as he folded his hands behind his back and started pacing. He didn't take his eyes away from mine. "Food supplies are dwindling at an alarming rate."

Each step he took seemed timed and perfectly calculated. It was as if he'd given this exact same speech before. And not just once, many times.

He lowered his head and looked away from me as he took four steps in one direction before pivoting and turning back to take four more in the other direction. Bobby Lee stood several feet behind him with his arms crossed in front of his bulky chest.

For two men who claimed food was hard to find, they looked rather meaty. In fact, they looked healthier than anyone I'd seen in a very long time. What they were doing here didn't seem like something they recently started because food supplies were vanishing.

My heart started to pound against my chest like it wanted to escape my body and get out of this room while it was still beating. I wondered if I was having a heart attack. If I was, it would probably be better than dying the way I imagined I was going to.

"Bobby Lee here and I, well, we found a way to solve all of our problems." Cy hit the end of his step, clicked his heels together, and stopped so he could grin at me. His eyes looked so dark, I could almost see the evil pooling up inside of them. "You'll be happy to know our plan is working perfectly. Bobby Lee and I couldn't be more thrilled at how successful our little thing has been."

"I'm so happy for you. Now let me go," I cried out as I twisted my wrist, not caring about the little streams of blood I could feel dripping down my arms. The cuts barely hurt, and I didn't give a thought to my burn injury. Was my body starting to go numb? Was it turning off so I wouldn't feel what they'd do to me? Somehow I doubted that possibility.

"Well, we can't do that now. You see, you and your friends out there, are an integral part of our plan. And all the other stupid folks that come snooping around here," Cy said with a practiced chuckle. He looked over his shoulder at Bobby Lee as if it was a reminder to join in, and of course Bobby Lee instantly started laughing too. I wondered if every time they did this routine, did Bobby Lee forget to laugh along?

When Cy's dreadful laughs stopped, so did Bobby Lee's. It was as though they had practiced the ending time and time again. Perfectly choreographed so they'd stop at the exact same moment and Cy could go on with his spiel.

"When we saw the six of you walking up, we knew we had been blessed. We'd won the jackpot. Food for weeks!" Cy's lips curled upwards showing his long, yellow teeth. I felt like I was being looked at by a hungry wolf and I was a poor defenseless little bunny.

I screamed so loudly I was sure that they could hear me in the shed. Only they were probably still out cold and couldn't hear anything at all. Or maybe if they could hear me, they couldn't move their bodies. I had no idea what these monsters had given them.

None of it mattered anyway. If they could hear me, they were still locked inside the shed. I was on my own and there wasn't anything I could do but try to accept my fate, but my mind wouldn't let me give up. It kept trying even though I knew it was pointless.

I pushed away from the wall and kicked around wildly. There wasn't a single thing I didn't do to try to break free from the old chains that held me. My raging outburst used up every bit of energy I had left. I was so weak I couldn't even hold myself up. My body hung from the wall like a sad, pathetic little rag doll.

Even though it was diminishing, I could still feel the slightest burning pain from the little cuts and the stinging from my burn. As long as I could feel them, even a little, I knew I was still alive. I hadn't given much thought to how I'd leave this world, but I was pretty sure this was the absolute last way I wanted to go. After everything I'd been through, I didn't want to be these two monsters' dinner.

"What about that guy yesterday?" I said so softly I wasn't sure if either of them had heard me. And I wasn't even sure if I cared. Why did it matter?

"Hmm?" Cy said, cupping his hand around his ear and leaning slightly in my direction.

"The guy yesterday… you just took him. You must have enough food that you don't need me yet," I said, my stomach turning at the thought of being their meal. I couldn't even believe those words had come out of my mouth.

Cy leaned back against the counter and dragged his thumb across his bottom lip. I felt like he was trying to show me that the taste of the guy was still lingering on his lips.

He shook his head, "That kid was just skin and bones. He probably would have died out there on his own in a day or two. There was nothing left on him."

"Tasted too much like beef jerky," Bobby Lee said, clearly not as pleased by the taste of the guy as Cy had been.

"Ha! Indeed, he did. That moron had been wandering around by himself out here without anything. He practically walked himself inside the shed," Cy said, tapping his palm against his forehead.

"Idiot," Bobby Lee added unnecessarily.

"He said he came with friends…," I said narrowing my eyes at them.

They looked at one another and laughed again. Bobby Lee held his stomach as he leaned back, looking as jolly as Santa but as evil as Satan.

"Yeah, imaginary ones!" Bobby Lee said between his slowing laughs. He looked at Cy as if he was waiting for a high-five.

I scraped my bottom lip with my teeth. My eyes darted around frantically and stopped on a blood stain on my bandage. It made me realize how desperate people were getting. No one valued another's life any more. Talking and begging wasn't going to get me out of these shackles. Nothing would. My blood would soon be mixed into the blood from the others that was splattered around decorating their wall and floor.

"Enough of this nonsense," Cy said as he reached over and picked up a medium sized ax. The blade was maroon tinged with the blood of those who'd been murdered before me. I couldn't help but wonder how many others there had been. Who were they? What had their lives been like? "Don't worry, this will be quick and painless. Wait, I'm wrong… you'll definitely feel it, but eventually you'll pass out."

Cy's expression changed slightly, and he stopped moving. He looked serious and rested the ax against the side of his leg. His eyes darted towards the ceiling and he folded his hands together so they pointed upwards.

"Let's not forget to thank Him for his

glorious bounty. Bless us, Oh Lord," he said as Bobby Lee closed his eyes and joined in. I squeezed my eyes together so tightly I was able to fuzz everything so much I couldn't hear Cy's words.

When I couldn't hear any mumbling through the haze in my brain, I opened my eyes to see Cy lifting the ax and moving towards me once again. His expression turned back into the crazed, hungry one I'd seen before.

Bobby Lee took a step forward and tilted his head, "Well, hold on there now, Cy. I've thought of something."

"What is it?" Cy growled. He was already licking his chops imaging what my cooked flesh would taste like smothered in their barbecue sauce.

"Well, it's not so often we get one this pretty, Cy," Bobby Lee said almost blushing. He glanced at me timidly and I saw that he too looked hungry, only his appetite was for something completely different. "We could keep this one for something else."

I wanted to scream again, but I couldn't find my voice. Cy looked like he was considering it. Death would be better. Being their meal would be better. I was in hell.

Chapter fifteen.

Cy looked at Bobby Lee and then at me. It appeared he was giving Bobby Lee's proposal serious thought. After several seconds he shook his head, and I actually felt relieved.

It seemed as though Cy's stomach had won out over the other thing he was considering. He drew closer, moving slowly, almost as if he was afraid I might bite him.

"There are two other girls out there for you, and that pretty boy too… I'll let you have your pick of one of those," Cy said as he gripped the handle of his ax tighter. He approached me as if I was a wild animal, but there wasn't much of anything I could do since I was chained to their wall of horrors. I felt weak, even though my mind still searched for escape, my body had given up. Cy looked directly into my eyes and he could probably see the disgust I had for him looking back. "Or all of them if you want!"

Bobby Lee grinned and took a step to the side so he could have a better view of what Cy was about to do with the ax. My heart was pounding so fast and so hard I thought I was going to pass out. And I was certain it would be better if I did.

Cy was so close I could smell his putrid body odor. They had water for drinking but they apparently didn't bother wasting any of it on cleaning themselves.

He lifted the ax and something inside my flipped. I don't remember even thinking about it before I thrust my leg forward and kicked him as hard as I could manage in the groin.

Cy doubled over and I pressed my back against the wall. I kicked my right leg upward wrapping it around his neck, as I swung my other leg up and twisted it around the other side. Then I squeezed my calves together as hard as I could.

My movements not only surprised me, they surprised Cy as well. He dropped the ax as both hands reflexively reached up to try to peel my legs away from his neck. I watched as it fell towards the floor. It seemed as though it was happening in slow motion as the blade slid alongside his leg and landed on his foot.

The blade must have been sharp because he squealed as the blood started to gush out of his boot. Cy's lips moved, but no words came out. He tried to find his voice and eventually choked out an order, "Get her... off me!"

Bobby Lee glared at me as he bared his teeth like a rabid animal. His feet pounded against the floor hard as he came rushing towards me.

This was it. My body wasn't going to react in the same way it had when Cy came at me with the ax. There wasn't anything I could do against the both of them while chained helplessly to the wall.

I was about to close my eyes and let everything happen when the door flung open so hard it hit the wall behind it with a clanging thud.

At first I was worried it was going to be more of them coming to help so they could all feast on me. They'd all just start angrily gnawing on my raw flesh while I was still alive. But it wasn't more of them, it was Penn.

He methodically walked towards the men, grabbing one of their solid dining room chairs as he passed by the table. Penn raised it up over his head and crashed the chair down over Cy's head.

His eyes rolled back, and he dropped to his knees. Penn must have spotted the knife on the counter, because in a matter of seconds he yanked it out of the cutting board and threw it across the room hitting Cy in the side of the neck.

When Cy reached up and started feeling the knife, Penn was already in front of him with his fingers gripping the handle. Cy's eyes looked blank, he didn't seem to understand what was going on. I looked away, not wanting to see Penn finish what he'd started.

Bobby Lee stood there staring, his eyes filling with fear. It was like he didn't know how to function without Cy telling him what to do. He started to slowly back away when Dean and the others entered the room, blocking his exit.

"I told you guys to wait outside," Penn said sounding exasperated, but he probably just didn't want them to see the bloodbath. Or get caught up in something dangerous.

I watched as the expression on Bobby Lee's face shifted to one of aggression. It looked like he was going to try to plow his way through the door and bowl over anyone that got in his way.

"On the table!" I shouted and Penn's eyes shot across the room to the table of guns. He started to make his way towards them, but Carter picked up one of the guns and didn't hesitate.

He raised the gun and pointed it at Bobby Lee. Bobby Lee didn't stop moving. Carter took several bold steps as he moved towards our captor. Bobby Lee changed his direction slightly and was about to launch himself at Carter when I heard the loud pop of the gun. Followed by another.

Bobby Lee froze in place as his anger vanished and turned into sadness, and then to complete devastation. He flopped to the ground as the life left his body.

Carter walked over to Cy and shot him, even though I was pretty sure he was already dead. I guessed he just wanted to be sure he was really dead.

Carter handed the gun to Penn. Penn nodded and looked the gun over before he stuffed it into the back of his pants.

"Get the guns," Penn instructed and Dean started sorting through the guns on the table. He took his and, presumably, mine. Dean didn't put them away, rather he held them and leaned against the doorframe as he watched and waited for others that may have been alerted by the gunshots.

Carter went to the table and helped himself to the rifle that I guessed had been Bobby Lee's. Cy had a gun, but apparently it hadn't been left on the table.

"Look around for Cy's gun," I said as my eyes quickly darted around the room. He must have hidden it somewhere, but I didn't know where.

Carter walked towards the side of the counter and raised a second rifle. "Here it is," he said, but he checked it over and shook his head.

"What is it?" I asked.

"It's empty."

There were no words for how I felt. I just wanted to get out of this hell hole as fast as possible.

"Don't forget about me," I said shaking my arms so the chains would rattle. Carter, Dean and Penn were armed, if anyone came around and ambushed us, at least we could fire back. Although I was pretty sure the guns were all low on ammo. Most importantly, if others did come I didn't want to be chained to the wall when it happened.

Penn bent down and started going through Cy's pockets. He pulled up a keyring with more keys than I could count. They were all different shapes and sizes... it would take forever to find the right one. For all I knew the right one wasn't even on the keyring.

Penn examined the shackles and then yanked on the them to test how sturdy they were. He frowned slightly and looked down at the keys, "Hmm... I'm not sure which one."

"Any of them look like they might be old or rusty?" I asked as I watched him scan through the assortment of keys.

"Not really," he said picking one at random and tapping it against the lock, but it wasn't even close the right size.

"The big guy put me up here... check his

pockets too," I suggested feeling as though I was grasping at straws.

Penn was about to ask one of the others to look while he kept trying keys, but Alice was already digging inside Bobby Lee's pockets. She didn't even look the least bit creeped out to be digging in the dead guy's pockets.

Alice shook her head as she moved from pocket to pocket, but then she pulled out a dirty, old looking key and ran over to my other arm. She slipped it into the hole and turned it. I wanted to cry when I felt the shackle pop open.

"Thanks," I said, as my arm dropped heavily to my side. It didn't even feel as though it was my arm. The muscles felt painful and stretched out. I couldn't use my arm the way I normally did. I tried to move it up and down hoping to bring life back into it.

Alice handed Penn the key, and he released my other arm. Penn held my arm and scooped me up before I fell flat on my face. He saw the cuts on my wrists, and looked at them nervously, "How's your burn?"

"Still hurts, but I'm fine. Let's get out of here," I said stumbling as I tried to move each leg in front of the other. Penn put his arm under mine and helped me to Dean and Carter.

"Help her... I'm going to look around for things we can use," Penn said and dumped the bones out of the trash can.

He started moving around the room quickly. I watched as he tossed the condiments from the table inside the bin before Dean and Carter led me out of the building.

Penn was behind us before we were even ten steps away from the building. I was pretty sure everyone was extremely anxious to get out of this place. Even though no one had come after us yet, it wasn't worth it to poke around. If we ran into others, it could mean our lives.

As we made our way out of the camp, I saw the door of the shed, the shed they had been locked inside of. It swayed back and forth in the light breeze. Somehow they had managed to break the lock off and escape. Bobby Lee must not have secured the door as well as he thought he had.

"What did you find?" I asked trying to look inside the blood stained trash can.

"Not much," Penn said as he stepped in front of us and led us out of the fenced in area. It felt like my body was returning to normal even though my muscles were sore. I pulled myself away so that we could all move quicker. I felt unsteady, but I managed and when the car came into view, I ran towards it.

Penn pressed the trash bin against Dean's chest before he dashed to the driver's side door. "Get in!"

Everyone climbed inside the car as quickly as possible. Penn started driving away before Carter had even been able to close his door.

Dean set down the trash can between his legs and apprehensively started sifting through the items Penn had collected. He'd taken the ketchup, mustard, and barbecue sauce as well as three bottles of water and a kettle.

"Don't drink the water," Penn said as he glanced over at Dean. "Might be drugged."

"Right," Dean said with a nod.

"How did you guys get out of the shed?" I asked leaning forward slightly. I looked down at my cut up wrists. They weren't as bad as I had imagined. I had cuts and scrapes but nothing deep, the burn on my arm had been far worse.

"Luck. And lots of perfectly timed kicking," Penn said without taking his eyes off the road. He was driving much faster than he usually did.

Dean reached back for my hand and when I took it I felt overwhelmed. I had to bite my lip to hold back my tears. He didn't look at me. "When I woke up and you weren't there…," Dean said his voice wavering, he paused and then he cleared his throat. "Well, that was my motivation to get the fuck out of that prison."

"Then that scream we heard. I was sure it was you," Sienna said rubbing my back. I couldn't turn to look at her because I knew I would definitely start crying. It didn't escape me how lucky I was to even be sitting in this car. In fact, maybe I was just imagining that I was here. Maybe I had died, but this was what I was telling myself had happened instead. It felt too good to be true.

"All I know is that we are never stopping anywhere ever again. We're on our own," Dean said squeezing my hand.

Penn nodded, "Agreed."

Alice rested her head against the window. It seemed as though the whole adventure had completely worn her out, or maybe it was just the after effects of whatever the men had slipped into their water.

The sun was hanging low in the sky and I was beyond exhausted from what I had been through, but I knew finding sleep would be difficult. I didn't have to ask to know that Penn was going to drive through the night.

Now that we had the kettle we'd only have to find a source of water. And maybe where there was water we could also find fish. Even though I hated fish, I'd have to learn to like it. Or at least learn to be able to keep it down. I was pretty sure that if there was a big, stinky fish in the car, I would have eaten some.

Alice started coughing before she settled herself against the window again. I could tell by her pallor she wasn't getting better. In fact, I was pretty sure she was getting worse.

When she was back at her resistance camp, she probably had the option of laying down and resting. But now that she was out with us there was very little chance to rest.

Sienna broke the silence with her own coughing fit. I slowly turned to look at her. She covered her mouth and held up her other hand to show she was OK. When she was finished, she smiled and shook her head, "Swallowed funny."

I couldn't help but wonder if she was coming down with the same cold Alice had. After all, out of all of us, she had spent the most time near Carter and Alice. I wondered if she could see the worry in my eyes, "Sure you're OK?"

"I'm fine! Promise!" Sienna said, and nestled back into Carter's arm with a smile on her face. He looked down at her and I could see how much he cared about her. In a world of crap, she found something that made her happy.

I was glad we had Carter with us. He'd helped take Bobby Lee out. He'd probably also helped them escape from the shed.

Carter cleared his throat and then closed his eyes as he rested his head against the top of hers. I turned to face the road as we sped down the highway. My breath was still weird and my muscles sore, but I was happy we were back out on the road searching for our private sanctuary.

Chapter sixteen.

Penn continued driving through the night just as I knew he would. He switched with Dean once when he couldn't keep his eyes open. We continued with only one stop to check an abandoned car on the side of the highway. After a few hours of Penn shifting around in the passenger seat trying to get sleep, he switched back to driving.

We had stopped at various locations along the way while the sun had been up. Everything along the highway had pretty much been cleared out. The only thing we found that was useful was a lighter, and it worked maybe one time out of ten.

Every so often we'd get a little gas from a car, but it would only give us a few miles before we'd need to find more. But we'd found enough to drive through the whole night and a good portion of the day.

We'd look for food, medicine, bandages, anything and everything we thought might be useful, but everything we checked was empty. And Penn was too anxious to wander into places that had once been towns or cities, afraid they had been taken over by HOME, the resistance, or some other crazy group of people.

We still had our supplies that we'd taken from the hotel and from the military base but it wasn't enough. The snacks were running low, and we still hadn't come across a source of water.

Alice seemed to get sicker with every mile, but there wasn't much we could do for her other than let her rest and try to find food, water and medicine. We'd driven for several hours and we hadn't found any gas to fill up with, so when the car slowly rolled to a stop, I knew why.

"Out of gas," Penn announced, but no one seemed the least bit surprised. During the night we had passed through the mountains and now everything around was flatland. The grasses and trees around were mostly dull green and brown. Without having seen a sign, I knew one thing was true, we weren't in Michigan.

With how flat everything was I could see for miles, and there wasn't a building in sight. Wherever we were had probably been hit by the tornadoes too, but something told me it hadn't been well populated before the storms either.

"Is she going to be OK to walk?" Penn asked Carter.

"I'll be fine," Alice said narrowing her eyes at Penn. "I'm just thirsty… and hungry, like everyone else."

"Sure, yeah," Penn mumbled as he got out of the car and went around back to look at our supplies. I watched as he coiled the hose around his shoulder. If we found a car, it would come in handy. Dean and Carter joined him at the back, each grabbing something to help out. Penn pulled out his gun and started leading us away from the road.

I was pretty sure it wasn't a good idea to abandon the road completely, but it was also probably a good idea to stay off of it, so we wouldn't easily be spotted. There wasn't much of anything to hide behind out here if someone approached.

Dean carried the trash can with the water bottles, condiments and kettle packed inside. Carter had it a little easier, he had his new rifle over one shoulder and the supplies in the garbage bag from the hotel over the other. My muscles were still sore or I would have offered to help them.

As we walked, we ate our snacks and

sucked on sugar. We were too hungry to worry about rationing what was left of our snacks.

We had walked for what I guessed had been a few hours. It was hard to keep track of days or time because each day seemed to bleed into the next. The erratic sleep schedules really messed with our body clocks.

"Water!" Penn shouted over his shoulder. He was about twenty feet ahead of us scouting the area as we walked. He was already gathering up supplies to start a fire by the time I caught up to him.

It was a small creek that was barely even there, but the water was gently flowing. I didn't know how long it would take to gather up enough to boil, but at least we'd found water.

We probably should have followed the creek for awhile to see if the amount of water would increase, but we didn't bother. Maybe Penn was worried about getting too far off course.

For now we had a few snacks, our condiments and maybe I'd be able to find some of that wild spinach again. Or maybe Carter and Alice knew of some other wild plants we could eat.

"Alice and Ros, you guys are going to sit this one out," Penn said as he handed Sienna the pitcher from the hotel supply bag and Dean the kettle.

"I'm fine. I want to help," I said, planting my hands on my hips. For the most part I was fine, although maybe I hadn't full recovered mentally yet.

"Me too," Alice said, unable to hide the coughing fit that started.

Penn smirked and shook his head, "Just rest up... both of you."

He whispered instructions to Sienna as if he was afraid we might overhear and take over her job. I heard him tell her exactly how he wanted her to gather the water using the pitcher. Once they collected enough, Dean would boil it in the fire using the kettle we'd taken from the military base. Carter paced back and forth watching one side while Penn stood up and paced the other, even though they would have seen someone coming for miles.

I watched Dean as he poured the water Sienna had given him into the kettle and set it on a big rock in the middle of the fire. Before anyone else could do it, I reached forward and pulled out the plastic bag that was filled with Styrofoam cups.

Dean noticed and pulled them towards his leg. He opened the bag and took out one of the cups and started etching something into the side of one of the cups carefully. Without having seen it, I was pretty sure he was marking which cup would be Alice's.

A blanket of clouds covered the sky, and it was starting to get dark by the time Dean finished boiling enough water for all of us to each have a full cup. Sienna dropped the empty pitcher on the ground near the fire and sat down next to Carter. She leaned her body into his with a big sigh.

"Well that was exhausting," she groaned.

Dean wiped his forehead with the back of his hand. His hair was damp with sweat from sitting so close to the fire for as long as he had, "Tell me about it."

Penn crouched down between Dean and I, but kept his eyes out towards the horizon. His voice was hoarse, "We'll stay here for the night."

He organized the sleeping plan, checked the guns and started walking the perimeter. We had an additional gun, and although I didn't know how many bullets were in it, I knew there weren't many.

Dean put his arm around me and pulled my body against his. He hugged me hard, and he didn't care in the least who was watching. Sienna and Carter were off in their own little world and didn't even seem to notice. Alice turned over on her other side and tucked her arm under her head for a pillow.

"I was so worried," he whispered into my ear before he kissed my neck and ran his hand lightly down my side. "I don't know what I would do without you."

"You'd keep fighting," I said, pursing my lips so tightly they felt like they could crack. "We are going to keep fighting and keep going no matter what. Right?"

He eased away feeling the tension in my tone and in my body. I was frustrated with everything. We'd fought so hard every day to get to where we were, I wanted to make it clear that if anything ever happened to either of us, the other had to keep going.

Sienna must have heard the end of our conversation. Maybe I had been louder than I had intended. She stared at us, "Agreed. If anything happens, we keep going. If any one of us ever gives up, we'll all lose."

I nodded in complete agreement. Dean looked back and forth and then pulled me back against him as if he understood. It would be hard, but we'd have to keep moving forward. Always keep moving forward.

* * *

When I woke up the sun was breaking over the horizon. I had taken my turn during the night but it had gone by without a hitch. No one was out wandering around in the middle of the night out where we were.

Sienna and Penn were at the creek working together to gather up more water. Carter, Alice and Dean were still asleep, but my moving around was causing Dean to stir.

I looked down at him as he slowly opened his eyes. His lips curled up on one side forming an irresistible and super sexy smile, "Well, what a beautiful sight to wake up to."

I could feel the pinkness filling my cheeks. It felt good to hear that, even though I probably looked like I'd been to hell and back.

"Come here," he said as he pulled me down on top of him. Dean curled his fingers around my neck and I shivered at his touch. His eyes were filled with a fiery intensity that was almost too much to look at. It was like looking at the sun, so bright I had to look away.

When our lips touched, I felt his desire. He kissed me as if no one was there. And it was filled with so much passion and need that I forgot where we were. I kissed him back and pressed my palm into his chest, slowly dragging it down his body.

Someone coughed and Dean clamped his hand down on top of mine. He had to stop things now, or maybe he wouldn't be able to stop them at all. We had to put a lot of things in our relationship on hold as we struggled to survive this cruel world. But I wanted him in every way possible and I could both see and feel he felt the same way.

We looked into each other's eyes and it was strange how I could see both the love he had for me, and a sadness. I hugged him and kissed him on the cheek before I got up to find something to eat.

We finished off the snacks and drank the water that had been gathered. Penn packed up our supplies, putting everything in the garbage bag. Since the trash can was awkward to carry without handles, we decided to just leave it behind.

"Ready?" Penn said as he yanked the bag over his shoulder.

"Let me carry that," I said thinking about how if one of us should have access to their gun at any given time, it should probably be Penn. Although, Carter had done just fine with one back at the military base.

Penn shook his head and kept moving forward. I don't know if he thought I was still too injured from what happened, but I was fine. My burn hurt more than the little cuts around my wrists, although my muscles were still a little sore.

It wasn't worth arguing about. The terrain was so flat that we'd see someone approaching from a mile away. He could just set the bag down and do whatever needed to be done.

Penn led the way staying about twenty feet ahead of us at all times, but he'd frequently look back. Dean and I walked together and Sienna, Carter and Alice brought up the rear.

Alice coughed, "Is there any of that medicine left?"

It was just some generic headache medicine so I couldn't imagine it helped much with her cough. Her illness seemed to get worse every day instead of getting better. It was most likely due to the fact we never stopped moving. I hoped we'd find a house soon. Take a few days off before we start up towards Michigan again.

"Penn!" I shouted as I started running towards him. When I was about five feet away he stopped moving to look at me. "Any of that medicine left? Alice is asking for it."

Penn started going through the bag, and then his pockets. Either we'd lost it or it was gone. He shook his head and shouted, "Sorry, Alice… it's gone."

"She's getting worse," I whispered, and he nodded.

"Yeah, I know."

"If we can find somewhere to stay for a few days… she just needs to rest up," I said looking around the horizon hoping to spot something in the distance.

"Let's keep moving," Penn said and jogged to get back ahead of me.

I stood there waiting for Dean and the others to catch up. When she coughed again, I wanted to help her, but there wasn't anything I could do.

"Sorry," I said looking back at her.

"Well that sucks!" she said and then cleared her throat. She looked at me as though she thought maybe I had done something with the medicine, or that I was keeping it all for myself.

I ignored her, "Let's keep moving." I turned my back to her, and she started coughing again, only this time she wasn't alone.

Sienna started coughing too. And it sounded like the same barking cough that Alice had.

Chapter seventeen.

"I'm fine… it's just, well, I was clearing my throat is all," Sienna said quickly trying to hide another cough. I pressed my lips together and sighed. There was no doubt in my mind Sienna had caught the cold.

We were all probably going to get the damn thing before long. It was even more imperative we find somewhere we can stay. If we all got sick, we wouldn't want to be out traveling about, we'd want to stay somewhere and get healthy before we made our way to Michigan.

"Do you feel OK?" Dean said looking at her with concern in his eyes. "You look pale. Doesn't she look pale?"

"I feel fine," she said putting her hands on her hips. "It's just a little tickle in the back of my throat. Probably just a dry throat from thirst."

Dean turned to Alice and lightly put his hand on her shoulder. Her eyes looked over at his hand and then back up at him. I could have been wrong, but I thought I saw all the sickness exit her body as her eyes filled up with pink hearts.

"What are your symptoms?" Dean asked.

"Well, there's this cough you may have noticed," she said, raising her eyebrow. But then she exhaled and I could tell she was trying to shake off her attitude. "Cough, sore throat, occasional chills, my chest feels tight and sometimes it feels like my heart is racing, even when I'm not doing anything. Oh, really bad headaches too. Not all the time but sometimes. I think it's related."

"Sounds like a bad head cold," Dean said looking at me as he shrugged.

I shrugged back, "A head cold with a really, really unusually bad cough. How long did you say you've had it for? A couple weeks?"

"Look!" Carter said pointing ahead. I shot him a quick glance. He shifted his eyes towards me for only a split-second. It felt as though he was intentionally trying to distract me… I was almost sure of it. Maybe she had been sick longer or maybe it had been worse than they let on. "Penn found a house."

Dean and I ran to catch up to Penn who was walking slowly as he approached the house. He adjusted his grip on his gun, and the look on his face was one of concern. Who knew what we were walking into? For all we knew there was someone inside and they could start shooting at us.

It looked like an abandoned ranch. There were a couple barns and a large farmhouse all surrounded by a wooden fence. From where we were the whole property looked to be in fairly good condition, which probably only worried Penn more. That maybe someone was taking care of it.

I glanced back feeling excited and optimistic until I heard the coughs behind me. My smile turned into a frown knowing it wasn't Alice. Carter was holding Sienna while she coughed. He was trying to block her from our view. Even Alice looked concerned, or maybe she was feeling bad that she had spread her cold.

"Shit," I whispered. Penn looked at me, his eyebrows pressed inward. "Sienna."

Penn and Dean both looked back and likely saw the same thing I had seen. Dean didn't say anything, but I could see he looked beyond worried.

I didn't think for one second that whatever Alice had was just a simple cold. She'd had it for a long time with no improvement. In fact, it seemed to have gotten worse in the short time she'd been with us. And Carter didn't seem surprised. It didn't take a doctor to figure out it was worse than the common cold. I wondered if Carter had seen others in their resistance camp get sick too. I wondered what happened to them.

"Let's hope this place is empty," Penn said taking a deep breath and moving forward towards the fence. He took a few running steps and launch himself over it as he moved quickly towards the house. Dean and I maneuvered over the fence in a much less graceful fashion.

The others caught up and Carter helped both Sienna and Alice over before he put his palm down and kicked his legs over like a gymnast. We followed Penn right up to the porch of the farmhouse.

I was surprised that bullets hadn't flown through the air at us while we approached. Penn didn't bother to knock. His fingers gripped the metal doorknob and tried to twist, but it barely moved. It was locked.

Carter stepped forward and looked down at

the doorknob. He looked as though he knew what he was doing, but instead of doing something to the doorknob he lifted the potted plant to the side of the door and revealed a shiny key.

He opened the door and pocketed the key. Inside the house it was completely silent except for a distant squeaking that sounded like something swing back and forth, like a door or a gate.

Carter shut the door once we were all inside. I heard the small click of him locking the door. Sienna clapped her hand over her mouth and I knew she was trying to stifle a cough.

Penn waved his hand at us to indicate we should stay in the living room as he crept forward with his gun stretched out in front of him. This house was bigger than others we'd stayed in. If he intended to check the whole thing himself, it would take forever. There was a second story and probably a basement too, not to mention the buildings outside.

He turned a corner but after a few seconds he came back. His face was all scrunched up, "A body near the kitchen."

I heard the squeaking noise again and worried it wasn't a door or a gate after all, but maybe someone creeping around. I pulled out my gun nervously.

"Help me move it outside," Penn said looking at Dean and then back at Carter. Penn turned around and stopped abruptly, "Shit!"

I peered around him and at the same time I heard the familiar growl of a dog-beast. The dog started slinking out of the kitchen slowly but

181

stopped to stare at us.

This dog-beast was twice the size of the others I'd seen. Not only heavier, but also it seemed taller. I swallowed hard at the red-tinged saliva that dripped down out of its mouth.

A second one, more normal sized, stepped out and bared its teeth. Penn put a bullet into the big dog and then one into the smaller one. The shots were perfect, and both dogs collapsed to the ground about a second apart. Then I heard the squeaking noise again.

"Is there a door open in there?" I asked looking around to see another dog had entered.

"Cover me," Penn said as he maneuvered over the dead dog-beasts, and I heard another shot, follow by another squeak. "Help me!"

Dean and I carefully stepped over the dog-beasts with our guns drawn. We entered the kitchen and saw the dead body of a man on the floor and a third dog-beast standing just outside of the back door.

Through the window I looked across the farmland. Approximately a hundred yards away were dozens of dog-beasts. They were just standing there and it felt like they were all waiting for something.

"What are we going to do?" I asked stepping behind the long curtain at the side of the back door so the dog-beasts outside couldn't see me.

"We have to get the body, and the dead dogs outside," Penn said.

There were three dogs huddled around something thirty yards from the back porch. The dogs stopped what they were doing to look up, and I saw they were feasting on another human body.

It seemed as though people had been living here until it was taken over by the dog-beasts. Somehow they must have gotten inside the fence and there wasn't anything the people could do about it. They must have been running for the house and didn't make it.

"The guy first," Penn said and grabbed the man's boots. He started dragging the body towards the door as Dean covered him.

"I'm not sure about this," I said ready to pull the door open. We hadn't even discussed the plan. It was as if we just somehow knew what to do after being together as long as we had been. "What if they attack?"

"It'll be fine. It's just a couple feet," Penn said rubbed his palms against his pants. "I think this will be the quickest way to get them out. I can do it without drawing their attention."

Penn counted and on three I opened the door. He pulled the body out fast and left it on the porch as he jumped over it to get back inside. I slammed the door shut, which seemed to alert the dogs. They charged towards the corpse.

"Lock it," Dean said, and I flipped the lock into place as I watched about twenty of the dog-beasts leap up onto the back porch and tear at the body. I stepped back behind the curtain so I couldn't see what they were doing.

"Are you sure these two are dead?" Carter said as he climbed over them and joined us in the kitchen.

"Pretty sure," Penn said barely glancing at them. "But I don't know what we are going to do with them. We can't leave them if we are going to stay here."

"You don't know what we are going to do with the dead dogs here, or all of those out there?" Carter said nodding towards the window. I could hear their loud gnawing and growls as they fought over every remaining morsel. Even though there was a wall between us I was still frightened.

"Both," Penn said, shaking his head. "I can't open that back door, and if we leave them in here they'll be stinking up the place in no time."

Carter nodded at the same time he let out a strange sputtering noise follow by a gulp. Then as if he couldn't hold it in any longer he let out a cough similar to that same hacking cough both Alice and Sienna had.

"Crap. Not you too?" I said, my hand reaching up towards his forehead like a reflex, but I froze in place when I heard the *creak-creak* of what sounded like someone moving around upstairs. "Another dog-beast?"

"I don't think so," Penn said, silently making his way to the stairs. He turned to Carter, "Stay with them. Dean... Ros... come with me."

It was nearly impossible to climb the stairs without them creaking and cracking with each step. Whoever, or whatever was up there would most definitely know we were coming.

At the top of the stairs was a gate about six feet tall with lock on the outside. I could see through the evenly spaced bars, but I wouldn't have been able to fit an arm through them. It looked as though it was some kind of homemade device to keep the upstairs and the downstairs divided.

Penn tilted his head and lifted a small lever type lock. It hadn't been there to keep something out… it was there to keep something inside.

Once through the gate there was a long hallway with three closed doors and two open doors. Penn opened the first door and moved his gun around, but it was just a linen closet, stacked with clean, precisely folded linens. The smell that wafted out was fresh and perfumey. It seemed so bizarre to smell these sweet, flowery fragrances in our dirty, stinky world.

He closed the door and moved to the next one, which was an open door. Penn stepped inside with his gun drawn. I followed him into the room holding my gun in the same way, except my safety was in place. Dean stayed by the door looking up and down the hallway, ready to use his gun should he need to.

It was a bedroom painted in whites and blues with a matching striped bedspread. The room was clean, and the bed was neatly made. Penn walked over to check the closet but it was empty.

"Under the bed," I whispered and Penn ducked down to check, but there wasn't anything under there. I nodded towards his gun, "How many do you have left?"

He didn't answer but instead lifted up one finger. If he needed more than one bullet for whatever was up here, Dean or I would have to assist. I would have just as well given him the bullets from my gun, but I knew he wasn't about to take the time to do that.

Dean stepped aside and covered us as we went into the next door. This room was made up just as neatly, and it was also empty.

There was a small squeak of a floorboard and Dean nodded towards the next room. We passed a door on our right. The door was open and we could see that it was a completely empty bathroom. No one could be hiding in there because there wasn't anything to hide behind, not even a shower curtain.

Penn slowly entered the next room, staying close to the wall. I followed, pointing my gun wildly as I pressed myself back, following his lead. It was as if I expected one of those dog-beasts to jump out at me. Although I didn't know how it would ever have gotten through that gate at the top of the stairs. My palms felt sweaty, and I was afraid I might drop my gun.

Then we heard another noise, and I knew without a doubt that it came from inside the closet. I pointed, but Penn had already figured it out. Probably before I had. He directed me to stand on one side of the door and with two fingers indicated he would pull it open.

First, he held up one finger, and then a second, and I knew when he reached down he was opening it on three. He pulled it open and stepped back waiting for something to leap out at him, but nothing happened.

We locked eyes, but he just shrugged. He looked around the door to peek in and shook his head side-to-side.

"We know you are in there… come out with your hands up!" Penn shouted in a deep voice.

"Yeah! Or we'll shoot!" I said. Penn looked at me with a raised eyebrow. The floorboards started to creak as whatever was inside of the closet started to move.

"Please don't kill me!" a soft voice whispered. She started sniffing, "Oh dear God, please don't kill me!"

Penn gripped his gun tighter and stared into the darkness of the closet. He lowered his voice again, "Are you armed?"

"Armed? Like with a gun?" she said as if she was offended by the question. "Of course I don't have a gun!"

"A knife? Anything that would be considered a weapon?"

"No," she answered with a sob.

Penn shook his head. He and I both knew better than to trust anyone, but for some reason I believed this girl. Even still, I wasn't about to lower my gun or let down my guard.

"Just come out slowly, with your hands up… we won't shoot," he said glancing at Dean. I couldn't see him, but I knew he was still in the hallway. If he would have left the area the floorboards would have given him away.

"Oh God, oh God, oh God," she mumbled, and I saw the clothing inside the closet shift to the side. I couldn't see much from my position but I could hear her slow, scared movements.

First, I saw her arm, and then a shoe

emerged. And then her other arm... she wasn't carrying a weapon. Her hands were shaking as she looked at Penn, not even noticing I was there. I took a step back, and she quickly looked over her shoulder at me. She screamed and stumbled forward as if I had startled her.

She was wearing dark blue jeans and a T-shirt that looked surprisingly clean compared to our wardrobes. I also noticed that she looked healthy. She wasn't skin and bones. It seemed as though she had been well fed.

"Oh... oh dear. Why...," she said crossing her arms and rubbing herself as if she was freezing.

She looked to be close in age to us, but what was she doing living out in the middle of nowhere alone? Then I realized she hadn't been alone. The bodies downstairs had probably been her parents.

"Why are you in our house?" she said looking at Penn and then at me. "Did my dad let you in?"

Chapter eighteen.

Penn looked at her. It appeared as though something about her confused him. He looked down at his feet for a second and then made his way over to the small window. The girl watched him as he gazed down at the yard, which I assumed was still covered with dog-beasts.

"When was the last time you talked to your dad?" Penn asked squinting, but it wasn't that bright outside.

She started to fidget, "You killed him didn't you? Oh fiddlesticks, I just knew it when I heard all those noises."

The girl tried to hold her face still, but it slowly scrunched up and quivered until she started sobbing into her hands. Penn looked at me with wide eyes and nodded towards her. I narrowed my eyes at him when I realized he wanted me to explain to her.

"We didn't kill your dad, or your mom, the dogs did."

"My mom's dead too?" She let out a howl as she clawed at her chest. "I should have known something was wrong when they didn't come up to see me."

I looked out her bedroom door, "You don't go downstairs?"

"Dad didn't allow it… safer up here. I've

been up here since the world ended," she said between whimpers.

"I killed the dogs that killed your parents," Penn blurted out as if he was afraid she still thought that we had come into her home and murdered her parents. She stopped crying to look at him with her wet eyes. Her eyelashes stuck together forming dark triangles as she blinked at him repeatedly. "I'm going to go downstairs now. Maybe Carter and I can get the dogs out the front door or something."

I rolled my eyes at this excuse. For some reason Penn was unable to communicate effectively or compassionately with this poor, isolated girl. She had no idea what hell was waiting down those stairs for her.

"What's your name?" I asked taking a step back. While she seemed harmless, I couldn't trust her enough to take my eyes off of her for more than a second.

"Lucy. What's yours?" she asked with a tiny smile showing mostly in her eyes.

"Ros."

"What's your friend's name?" she asked looking at her fingers.

"Penn," I said shifting my weight from one leg to the other. "You really haven't been outside since this all started?"

She shook her head side-to-side and smiled with her hands folded into her lap. I started to think that she hadn't been out much at all even before everything was destroyed.

"How did your family survive everything?

It looks like you all did very well for yourselves," I said looking at her again. She was tall and had at least twenty pounds on me. It wasn't at all that she was overweight, she was normal weight and I was far too underweight. Her hair was shiny and perfectly combed, and she smelled like soap and flowers.

She stood up and took an excited step towards me, but when I recoiled she put her palms up to show she had nothing. It was as if she realized she was coming on too strong. She flashed me a thin-lipped smile.

"My dad always said something like this would happen. You should see our basement!" she said as she hopped up and down quickly. She was far too energized. It was like she was on fast forward while the rest of the world was stuck on play, or maybe even pause. "Oh and those dogs… my dad was storing them in the barn out back in case we ran out of food. We were going to eat them!"

"Oh crap!" I said stepping back against the wall. Dean must have heard me hit the wall because he stepped inside the room holding his gun up towards the girl. "Did *you* eat any of them?"

"No, not yet. That was a backup plan. But looks like they all got out," she said with a small frown as she looked out the window. "You guys can have one. There is no way I'll be able to eat all those dogs by myself."

I shook my head and looked into her eyes as if she was slow, "Do not eat the dogs. Never eat the dogs."

"Well, why on earth not? Times are tough," she said squeezing her eyebrows together.

"Poison." The only word that I was able to get out of my mouth. I didn't know how to make it any clearer than that. There was no way any one of us would ever risk eating the dog-beasts.

"Well, we have other stuff downstairs... I guess I could share, since it's just me now. I worried about this day. The day I'd be alone. Of course I thought it wouldn't happen until my parents were much older," she sniffed and the tears started rolling down her cheeks again.

I walked over to the door to stand by Dean. The room was starting to feel a little stuffy, and I wanted to get downstairs. This girl, although nice, didn't seem entirely normal.

"Why did you think this would happen?" I asked almost not wanting to hear the answer.

"Mom and dad would fight about those dogs all the time. He wanted to keep as many as we could and they just kept coming! It was like they were looking for the missing and they'd send more. After my dad filled the one barn he started on the other one over there," she said pointing out towards a smaller building that looked like maybe it had been a stable. "But mom said we had enough and that he needed to stop taking them in. We could hear them growling at night... they were angry, fighting one another and I'm pretty sure they'd eat one another too, but dad told me I had a good imagination."

I shivered just thinking about all those horrid dog-beasts clustered inside of the barn. It wasn't the least bit surprising that they broke free and attacked her parents.

"Then the other day, they were fighting again, my parents that is, and I heard a banging noise followed by a loud crash. My mom stopped shouting at him after that. I called out to her, but she didn't answer, neither did my dad. After that, I heard the back door open and moments later another loud noise, and then the growls from the dogs. I ran to the window to see the dogs flooding out of the barn. They had broken free. I knew mom must have been so angry," she said twisting her fingers and scraping the tip of her shoe against the floor.

The only thing I could think about was how I was pretty sure based on what she'd just told me that her dad had killed her mom, but this girl was so innocent her mind hadn't even gone to that dark place. I felt bad for her.

In my mind I could see her dad dragging the mother's body out to the backyard, as he ran back towards the house, only he didn't make it. He hadn't even been able to close the door before the dogs got him.

"Every so often I heard the back door open and close, so I thought my dad was still down there, but he wouldn't ever talk to me. I guess, thinking back, that was a little weird." She shrugged and then wiped away a stray tear from the corner of her eye.

"May have been the wind… or the dogs. Because he was gone when we got here," I said looking at her clean shoes.

"Guess so," she said but then she started

smiling. I widened my eyes, surprised at the sudden change of her expression. "Can I go downstairs?"

I looked at Dean. She'd probably freak out if she saw the dog-beasts laying dead on the floor. I wasn't sure she'd be able to handle seeing all the blood.

"I'll go see if they are ready for us," Dean said stepping to the side. He paused and looked at me and then the girl. It seemed as though he was nervous to leave me alone. I was pretty sure I'd be OK unless she had an older brother that would pop out after Dean left, but that was probably pretty unlikely. I would have heard the floorboards moving somewhere by now.

Lucy and I looked at each other awkwardly as we waited for Dean to return. I couldn't think of anything else to ask her that she'd know the answer to. It seemed as though she was pretty oblivious to everything that had been going on around her.

It felt as though Dean was taking forever. I kept looking at the doorway hoping he'd appear.

"Are your parents dead too?" she asked looking at me as she laced her fingers together.

"I think so. After the storms I never saw my mom again," I started to look around her plain room to see if I could learn anything about her. I didn't want to talk about my mom with this strange girl. I didn't want to talk about her at all. There wasn't any point in talking about all that I had lost.

"What about your dad?"

"They were divorced. I barely ever saw him."

"Sorry to hear that," she said looking as though she wished she wouldn't have asked.

"Don't be. None of that matters anymore," I said using a tone that I hoped would convey my lack of interest in this conversation.

I was relieved when I heard someone coming up the stairs. I looked out the door and saw Dean heading towards us.

He stopped when he saw me looking at him, "You guys can come down now."

"Finally," I muttered and gestured for Lucy to follow me. She hopped and skipped as if I was taking her on a field trip. I was pretty sure once she saw the bloodstained carpet her mood would probably change.

When we got downstairs, and she saw all the others, she hid behind me shyly. I guess we should have warned her that it wasn't just the three of us.

"That's Carter, Sienna and Alice over there on the sofa," I said pointing them out as I said their names. "This is Dean and I'm sure you remember Penn."

She just smiled. I figured it would probably take her awhile to get used to all of us and learn our names. As long as she let us stay in her house, that was… although I wagered she would let us stay as long as we wanted. I didn't think she'd want to be left alone.

"Everyone, this is Lucy," I said trying to take a step to the side so they could see her, but she followed me. I saw her hand shoot up and give a little wave.

"Hi," she whispered quickly, but it was only

loud enough for me to hear. I sighed and walked over to the tell Penn about what she'd said about the supplies downstairs… she followed me like a lost puppy.

He turned to go check the basement, and I grabbed him by the arm. I handed him my gun, and he looked at me like I was crazy.

"No," he said firmly.

"Just switch." I shook the gun at him and shot him a look that hopefully conveyed that I wasn't going to take no for an answer. He groaned, but he took the gun and handed me his.

For all we knew it was some kind of trap. Maybe they stored more dog-beasts in the basement. Any kind of evil could be down there waiting. Clearly it was better for him to take the gun that had more bullets.

Penn gestured at Dean and Carter and they followed him down the stairs. Lucy and I went back to the living room where Alice was moving around on the sofa trying to get comfortable. Sienna was slouched in a chair looking more miserable than she had when I had left her to go upstairs.

I didn't know if the illness was hitting her fast or if she had given up on pretending it wasn't affecting her. Alice had been miserable as well. Maybe now that we were at Lucy's they could catch up on some much needed rest.

"Are they OK?" Lucy asked softly, not wanting them to hear her voice.

"They're sick," I said watching as Sienna leaned her head back and rested her forearm over her eyes.

"There are beds upstairs…," Lucy said looking sad. But then her eyes lit up. "We have medicine! My dad put it up high in the kitchen. I'll show you!"

She pulled me along. If she noticed the bloodstains she didn't comment on them. I couldn't tell but it looked as though she was forcing the smile to stay on her face. When her lip quivered, I knew she was trying to stay strong.

"Up there," she said pointing as she pulled one of the kitchen table chairs across the floor. We both jumped when there was a loud bang at the back door and then another at the window.

I saw the dog-beasts showing their teeth and growling at us as if we were food. They were still hungry.

I took a breath and walked right up to the window and closed the curtain, and then did the same to the one on the back door. They still growled, but at least I couldn't see them looking at me any more.

"Up here?" I said adjusting the chair.

"Yes ma'am," she said, her voice as sweet and gooey as honey.

"Ros."

"Right. Ros."

I wasn't quite tall enough to see everything in the cabinet, but off to the side was an array of cold and allergy medicines. I stood on my tip-toes and took out the liquid cold medicine. Before I brought it out to the living room I checked the dosing and measured out the first little cup. I handed the liquid to Sienna first and then, after she drank it all down, I poured out Alice's dose. It probably wouldn't matter if they shared the same little cup since they both had the same sickness.

"Thanks," Sienna said as she released a breath. She turned to curl up in the recliner.

I brought Alice her medicine, and she nodded her thanks as she closed her eyes. It was probably just as well to keep them down here so we were all together. At least until we figured out our plan.

"What happened to your arm?" Lucy whispered trying to be careful not to disturb Sienna and Alice from their rest.

"I got burned in a fire," I said rubbing at the bandage lightly. The bandage was in pretty sad shape and definitely needed to be replaced. It had a blood stain and all kinds of little threads were starting to fall out. Hopefully, we could find something around here that we could use to fix it. Perhaps there was a first aid kit somewhere.

Lucy looked scared. I wasn't sure she would ever be able to comprehend the world outside of the safe zone her parents had created for her. She wouldn't have that same safety any more because now she was all alone.

If her dad wouldn't have collected the dog-beasts for backup food, maybe none of this would have happened. Well, except for the part where her dad likely killed her mom, that might have still happened. But probably under different circumstances.

The boys came pounding up the stairs

breaking my train of thought. Dean came up first and looked at me, shaking his head, "You aren't going to believe this."

Chapter nineteen.

I followed them down to the basement. The stairs were old, knotted pieces of wood that felt as though they might not hold me.

The basement was filled with shelves and shelves of supplies. There wasn't much variety but there was a lot of things that must have been purchased in bulk. Either her dad knew this was going to happen, or he was prepping for any disaster.

"Can we take it?" I asked running my fingers across every can of soup as if I wanted to make sure they were real.

"Well, no, you can't take it," Lucy said with a giggle. "But you guys can all have some while you are here."

Was she going to kick us out? It wasn't like she'd want to stay here alone with the flock of dog-beasts roaming around outside her back door. Would she?

I assumed we'd get to stay here as long as we'd need to. It wasn't like we had to get anywhere by a certain time. This placed seemed as nice of a place as any other, well, except for the dog-beasts outside.

We hadn't seen any resistance since we picked up Alice and Carter, nor had we seen anyone from HOME. If either of them were in this area,

Lucy probably wouldn't have known, unless maybe she'd have overheard her parents talking about them. But if HOME was in the area, Lucy and her family wouldn't have still been here.

Penn scooped a bunch of cans off of the shelf and glanced at Lucy. She didn't stop him and instead she flashed him a sweet smile. He looked away and dashed up the stairs.

"Was that all just for him?" I said under my breath. Dean smiled as he looked down at me and pulled me around to the other side of one of the shelves.

When we were blocked from view, he tilted my head up towards his and kissed me hard. I wrapped my hands around his neck and leaned into him. If only we could stay down here away from the world forever.

"Come on," Dean said as he grabbed my hand and pulled me around. It was like we were shopping in a grocery store. He paused when he spotted the stacked cases of water bottles.

Dean dropped my hand and started to lift up one of the cases. Lucy clicked her tongue, and he turned to look at her.

"We drink the boiled water upstairs first. That's the emergency water. Let's go up!" She stared at us, taking each step slowly until we started to follow her up.

"Oh… um… all right then," Dean said looking at the water several times as if he couldn't stand the idea of leaving it behind.

"Go," I said pushing on his back lightly with my fingertips.

After we ate and drank until our stomachs puffed out, Penn asked about first aid supplies. Lucy showed him where they were and they brought everything out onto the kitchen table. Penn tended to my burn while the others relaxed in the living room.

I could hear the dog-beasts scratching around and growling at one another outside. The curtain was still closed so I couldn't see how many of them there were out there, but I was pretty sure it was a lot. The bodies of Lucy's parents and the dog-beasts had probably been completely devoured.

Penn used a piece of gauze to apply some of the antibiotic cream. I winced when the cool cream touched my hot skin. "How does it look?"

"Better," he said as he laid out several squares of gauze over the burn and carefully taped them down with the medical tape. "I'm not even sure you need this. I've had sunburns that have looked worse."

I wasn't sure if he was telling me the truth or if he was trying to make it seem better than it actually was so that I wouldn't worry about it. Either way I didn't want to look. I didn't want to see it. If I saw it, I'd only feel it more, this way it was easier to pretend it never happened.

"Did you find out anything useful from her?" Penn asked shifting his eyes towards the living room. I figured he was trying to gauge if Lucy was in earshot before asking anything too specific.

"No, not really, anyway," I said glancing over my shoulder. She was busy looking around the room as if she was discovering new things she'd never seen before. "She was kept up there for a long time it seems."

"That doesn't surprise me one bit," he said with a chuckle. He rested his elbows on the table and leaned forward as if he was waiting to hear more.

"And I think her dad killed her mom—"

"What?"

"I don't think it was the dogs," I said crossing my arms in front of my chest. Penn looked at me with wide eyes as I told him everything Lucy had told me about that day. He nodded along and seemed to agree with my assessment of what had happened.

"Guess he got what was coming to him," he said looking towards the window. He stood up and slowly pulled the curtain to the side and peered out. "Does she suspect her dad did it?"

"I don't think so."

After a few minutes, a dog popped up and slapped the window with its paw. We both jumped and the dog-beast started barking at us. Penn dropped the curtain and took several steps away from the window.

"What are we going to do about all of them?" I rubbed my new bandage lightly. My mind took over, and I could feel what it would have been like to have the dog-beast poison running through my veins. We had to do something about the dogs.

"I have no idea."

"Did you see how many were still out

there?"

"A lot," he said walking towards the door to make sure it was locked. It wasn't like the dog-beasts could figure out how to get inside, but he looked as though he was worried they might. "I think I have an idea."

I was fascinated by the growing grin on his face. Whatever he was imagining made him smile. I only hoped it would work.

I turned around and grabbed my heart when I saw Lucy was standing only about six inches away from me. How long had she been standing there?

"Lucy! Don't do that!" I said failing to keep the scolding tone out of my voice.

"Do what?"

"Sneak up on people. You scared the crap out of me!"

"Sorry! Why do you hate them so much?" she said. Her eyes were empty as if she knew they were bad but couldn't fully accept what we had told her about them. She didn't want to believe they were bad. Maybe she couldn't believe that anything, or anyone, was bad. She definitely wouldn't last very long outside of these walls.

"They are just very dangerous. If they bite you... well their poison will kill you," I said, leaving out all the parts about what happens before you die. I also left out the parts about HOME and their cure.

"Oh. Well... OK. Then I don't like them either," she said and turned on her heel. She left and returned to the living room. I watched as she poked at knick-knacks on the shelf.

Penn stood up and ran his fingers through his short hair, "Lucy? Come back in here for a second.

"Yes?" she said stepping into the room like a frightened little girl. It looked as though she thought she was going to get yelled at for touching the knick-knacks.

"Did your dad feed the dogs?"

"I don't think so, but sometimes they'd eat one another," she said with a frown. "He'd come in the house and I could hear him downstairs complaining about how many we'd lost."

"And how many did you lose?"

"I'm not sure." She frowned and shook her head.

"Hmm, OK," Penn said nodding. Lucy stood there looking back and forth between us as if waiting to be dismissed. Penn tapped his fingertips on the table when she didn't move, "Thanks... that's all."

Lucy turned her body stiffly and walked out of the kitchen. Penn stood up and starting pacing.

"This could actually work," he said rubbing his palms together, looking like a mad scientist.

I stood up and stepped in front of him to stop his pacing. He had a fiery determination in his eyes that was contagious. "OK, so what's your idea?"

* * *

Dean, Penn and I stood at the upstairs bedroom window looking down over the backyard. I wasn't sure if there were fewer of the dog-beast or not. It didn't really matter how many there were, what mattered was that there was still far too many of them. While they were out there we were stuck inside this house, whether Lucy wanted us here or not.

"This isn't going to work," Dean said crossing his arms in front of his chest. His pessimism was distracting and annoying Penn. We needed this to work, but unfortunately, Dean was probably right. And worst of all, there was a chance it would leave us with zero bullets either way.

Penn didn't want to use the gun Carter had taken from the military base, but he wanted the other three guns. I wasn't sure how many bullets were left in my gun, or in Dean's, but the one I now carried, that had originally been Penn's, only had one bullet left. Or at least that was what Penn had told me earlier.

If the plan didn't work, we'd just be out of bullets and all the dogs would still be there. But what choice did we have? As long as we were inside the house and the dogs knew it, they weren't leaving. I set down my gun on the nightstand near Penn and Dean did the same.

"Maybe it won't," Penn said as he unlocked the window and slid it upwards. He looked out as if he expected one of the dogs to jump up and into the window. When that didn't happen, he got down on a knee and started aiming up his first shot. "But let's hope that it does."

Penn rested his arm against the windowsill and held his breath. I jumped at the pop of the gun even though I knew it was coming. It sharply echoed throughout the room making my ears ring. I watched as the dog in the center of the pack took a few wobbly steps before going down on its side.

I couldn't tell if the dog was dead, but it was definitely wounded. The other dogs around it growled as if they thought they were being attacked. But when they couldn't find a threat, they turned to paw at the dog on the ground.

"Now to make them mad." Penn expertly aimed up a second shot. The bullet ripped across one of the dog's fur leaving behind a flap of torn flesh. The dog-beast turned on the dog behind him as if it had attacked him. It stretched out its paw clawing at the other dog's eyes. Then it launched itself towards the second dog's neck, aggressively digging its sharp teeth in and clamping down.

The other dog-beasts in the yard started to close in to see what was going on, or maybe they were just hungry and wanted their share.

Penn waited several minutes until most of the dogs had grouped together in the middle of the yard. He lined up another carefully calculated shot and seconds later another attack between the dogs broke out.

The plan was working. The dogs turned on one another. Several backed away looking as though they weren't going to get involved, but most of them were attacking.

Penn held off from firing out another round.

There was no point in using a bullet if he didn't need to. I wasn't even sure if the gun he was holding had any left. If he needed more he'd have to switch over to Dean's gun.

The savage attacks were too much to watch. Pools and splatters of dog-beast blood covered the ground. I stopped watching and went downstairs to check on Sienna and Alice.

Carter was sitting on the floor, the gun laying next to him and Sienna's head in his lap. He looked down at her as he stroked her hair behind her ear.

Alice had her back to them while she rested on the sofa. Her body slowly moved up and down, which I hoped meant she was actually getting some sleep.

"How are they doing?" I whispered as I looked down at Carter with my arms crossed.

He shrugged, "Still sick. It'll probably take a while for Sienna to fight it off since she only just caught it. But I hope her immune system is stronger than Alice's."

Carter stared at his sister's sleeping body. It looked as though he wished he could do something to make her feel better. He let out a sigh and pushed his face into his palm. It was hard for him seeing his sister, and now Sienna, going through this.

"I think the cold medicine helps some… at the very least it helps them get sleep," Carter said as he brushed a stray strand of hair away from Sienna's mouth.

At least when they were sleeping they

weren't coughing. I hoped he was right about Sienna's immune system, but with how little food and water we'd had over the last few days, weeks... months, I imagined Sienna was going to have the same struggles Alice did. She'd been in a camp where they'd been fed, or at least I assumed they had been, which was probably better than what we'd had.

I walked towards the kitchen to get myself a drink of water, when I heard noises at the front door. It sounded as though the door handle had been jiggled, but when I looked it wasn't moving. I glanced at Carter and he was gently moving Sienna off of his lap and reaching for the gun. He had heard it too.

Our eyes met. I wanted to go back across the room to get closer to him, but I felt frozen in place. I reached behind me for my gun, but it wasn't there. Penn had my gun upstairs.

Whoever was out there started talking. They seemed to be laughing. Why weren't the dogs attacking them? Hadn't they seen them? Maybe the dogs were just too busy fighting one another to even notice.

The door handle jiggled again, and I moved into the kitchen trying to hide behind the wall. I didn't have any way to alert Dean and Penn without the person outside hearing me. All I could do was hope that Carter was ready.

"Here. I found mine. Stupid," the voice said, close enough to the door that I heard every word. Then it sounded as though a key was being inserted into the doorknob, and I watched the knob turn as the door began to open.

Chapter twenty.

The door flung open and two boys stood there staring in at us. At first they looked confused, as if maybe they had walked into the wrong house, but it didn't take them long to realize they were in the right place and that we were the ones that didn't belong.

Their eyes darted around the room as they tried to take in what they were seeing. I was just happy they weren't shooting at us.

"Who are you?" the taller of the two said as he raised his shotgun. He was alternating who he pointed it at between Carter and I. He ignored Sienna and Alice even though they were starting to wake up.

"And what are you doing in our house?" the shorter one said squinting. He tried to look at us, but kept squinting as though we were too bright for him.

The shorter one copied the taller and raised up his gun. It looked as though he had it pointed at the wall behind me. Neither of them looked particularly comfortable holding a gun, but I wasn't going to risk being wrong about it.

I couldn't speak. When I heard someone coming down the stairs, I wasn't sure if I should be worried or relieved. I couldn't even look up to see who it was.

"Ahh! You guys are back!" Lucy squealed as she ran down the stairs. "I thought he sent you away forever and ever!"

Lucy gave the tall one a hug first and then moved over to the shorter one. They both looked at her as if she had been caught throwing a party while her parents were away.

"What's going on Lucy? Where's mom and dad?" the tall one asked and then shifted his eyes towards us. "And who are they?"

"These are my friends. They were out there and just happened to find our house. And it's good they did because I helped them," she said wrapping her arm around the taller guy's bicep.

"Did dad let them in?"

"No…." Lucy sniffed and then burst into tears. She couldn't hold it in even if she wanted to.

"Oh crap," the shorter one said raising his gun back up at us. "What did they do?"

"They didn't do anything," Lucy said, wiping at her tears.

Penn and Dean must have heard voices they didn't recognize because they quickly descended the stairs. Penn gestured for Alice and Sienna to stand behind him.

They both did as they were told, but they moved slowly. I wasn't sure they even knew what was going on. They were somewhere between their dreams and reality.

Dean spotted me by the kitchen and slowly made his way over to me. He secretly passed me a gun. I assumed it was the one that only had a single bullet left.

"Where's our dad?" the taller one asked between clenched teeth.

Lucy just shook her head as if she couldn't say the words. She pressed her face into his arm.

"Who let you out, Lucy? Was it them?" the shorter one asked.

"What do you even care? You left me! You left all of us!" Lucy fired back and then clapped her hand over her mouth as though she couldn't believe what she'd said.

Penn stepped to the side as if he was looking to see if we could squeeze out around them if things got bad. I was pretty sure we wouldn't be able to leave out of the kitchen, or we'd walk into an angry pack of dog-beasts.

I knew Penn was worried about what they were going to do once they found out what had happened to their parents. Even though we had nothing to do with it, they probably weren't likely to believe it.

"Dad?" the shorter one called out and waited for his dad to answer. Which I knew he wouldn't.

"He's dead!" Lucy screamed as she stepped away from them, hugging herself. "And mom is too!"

The taller one raised his gun and pointed it at Carter, probably because he saw that he was armed. If they made any kind of move Penn didn't like, and if he had two bullets left, this whole thing would come to an end. Lucy would not only lose her mom and dad... she would also lose her brothers.

"They did this? And you let them stay here? Lucy how stupid are you?" the taller one asked.

"No, of course not. But they found them. It was dad's dumb dogs that did it," Lucy said as the tears still streamed down her cheeks. There were so many tears the little droplets dripped down off of her jaw.

The taller one grinned, it almost seemed as though he was happy about the news. But I could tell by the look in his icy blue eyes that he didn't believe we had just found either of them that way. As far as he was concerned we were already guilty.

"I think it's time for your friends to leave," the tall one said gesturing at the shorter one. They stepped aside, opening a path between them to the front door. I was surprised when the dogs didn't race inside and feast on us all.

Lucy grabbed the taller one's arm and pulled on it, "There are too many of those dogs out there!"

"I don't care. It's time for them to go. They've overstayed their welcome," he said flicking the barrel of his gun once towards the door.

Penn lifted his arms and took a step towards the door. It felt like we had no choice. We could have tried to fight them, but they had guns too. It wasn't worth risking a bullet hole in one of us. We'd have to let the basement filled with food, water and supplies go. At least for now.

Maybe we should have fought. Maybe Penn could have taken them all out, but it just didn't feel right. It would be hard to continue on if we fought, and it led to one of us dying.

Leaving everything behind was hard. Who

knew if we'd ever find anything this good again? But if one of us got killed, it wouldn't be worth it. There were more supplies out there, we would just have to find them.

"Wait!" Lucy said and ran to the kitchen. She came back carrying a jug of water and shoved it towards Penn. "Take this. There is another farmhouse just up the road. I used to see cars go up that way at night but I haven't in a long time. Maybe there is help there!"

"What about our things?" I asked her, but her brother must have overheard.

"Ours now. And don't give them our water, Lucy!" the taller one scolded.

"Shut up, Thomas!" she screeched as she stomped her foot. "You left me here. This is my water and I'll do what I want with it. Why are you back anyway? I heard dad tell you to leave and never come back!"

The taller one, Thomas, just shook his head at her. "OK you got your water, now get off our property."

They must have come back because like everyone else out there they were struggling to survive. At least they had somewhere to come back to. We didn't have anything.

"All right, we're going," Penn said opening the door and stepping to the side to let us out while he covered us. Sienna, Alice and I walked out single file with Dean and Carter behind us. Penn watched them for any sudden movements as he came out last.

We stared at them looking out at us.

Waiting to see if they'd say anything more, but they didn't. The door slammed shut, and I heard the lock click into place. Carter reached into his pocket and held up the key. He smiled, but the key was practically useless. Sure, we could have used it to sneak in at night, but then if we didn't kill them, we'd always have to be watching our backs.

"Should I keep it?" Carter asked looking at Penn.

"Might as well," Penn said looking out at the horizon. I didn't know if he was looking for the neighboring farmhouse or looking for dog-beasts. "But we're going to keep moving. Michigan right?"

I smiled, even though I was thinking about all the supplies in the basement. At least we knew they were there.

I heard yelling inside the house. One of the boys, probably Thomas, was telling her how stupid she was for letting strangers in. And then the voices faded and I couldn't hear anything. Either they had made their peace, or they had brought her back upstairs and locked her up once again.

"Let's get out of here before the dog-beasts realize where we are," Penn said leading us away from the house. We had had a long way to go before we were out of sight of the house and the dog-beasts.

"How much ammo do we have left?" I asked tucking my gun into my waistband.

"Three in Dean's, one in mine and one in yours. Plus whatever Carter has," Penn said with a heavy sigh. It wasn't enough. I didn't know if it could ever be enough.

"And how many dog-beasts were left?" Carter asked adjusting his gun on his shoulder in case he had to use it. He turned around and walked backwards to keep us safe from behind.

"There were far more dogs than we have bullets," Penn said looking over his shoulder towards the house. "I think they are fenced in, although they could probably jump it. Let's go find that farmhouse."

The fence explained why the dog-beasts hadn't been roaming around in the front of the house. No one had even bothered to check, we just assumed they were everywhere.

"And let's hope that if anyone is there, they are super afraid of empty guns… well nearly empty anyway," I said combing my fingers through my knotted hair.

Sienna laughed, but it quickly turned into a coughing fit. She held up her palm when she saw me watching her. We had a jug of water, but we couldn't all drink from it. At least not without risking our health.

Penn gripped the jug of water tighter, as if he had the same thought. He didn't immediately head in the direction of the farmhouse, first we had to get out of sight. It was bad enough there were still so many of those dog-beasts left. Although, now there were fewer after Penn's experiment had worked. But if you asked me, one of those things was too many.

We walked for two hours before we found a farmhouse. Even though Alice and Sienna hadn't asked for a drink, our water was half gone. I wasn't sure if this place was even the one Lucy had been referring to, but at least we had found somewhere to stay.

If it was safe, we could spend the night, maybe two. Or perhaps, since Alice looked like a ghost, we could stay even longer. Just until Sienna and Alice were well again, although we'd have to find a water source and food, because the more we walked the more they coughed.

Penn took out his gun with the single bullet as we approached the house. This house was much smaller than Lucy's family's house had been. There was a small fenced in area that had a tiny building next to it that looked as though it had been for chickens. If only those chickens were still there.

We walked right up to the door and didn't waste any time going inside. I was happy to be indoors since the whole walk I couldn't stop looking in all directions, expecting a dog-beast to pounce on me and maul me to death. My eyes were strained and needed a break before they refused to continue working.

I wasn't sure, but I thought it would be better to face armed strangers over the wild dog-beasts. At least you could try to reason with people, whereas the dogs didn't care about that. They only cared about killing you, ripping you from limb to limb and filling their bellies.

Looking around the square living room I could tell how far into the country we were by how the home had been decorated. There were afghans draped over the furniture, and pictures of roosters and strange looking cow figurines. The room looked as though it hadn't been touched in months, with a thick dust coating everything.

It was as if I could tell the house was empty by how the air felt around me. If something jumped out at me, it would have been enough to give me a heart attack because I was so positive there wasn't anyone in the house. Well, and my heart probably wasn't very strong the way it was… it wouldn't take much.

"You guys stay here," Penn whispered pointing down at the floor in front of my feet. Then he pointed at Dean and then towards the kitchen, "Dean… you're with me."

We stood there barely moving and barely breathing as Dean and Penn started in the kitchen and moved around the house, carefully checking the rooms, closets and locks on the doors and windows. I wondered if everyone else had the same feelings I had about the house being empty. But even if there wasn't anyone inside of it now, that didn't mean it would stay that way.

After they finished checking the upstairs, Penn and Dean came back down. Dean collapsed into a chair and Penn let out a huge sigh.

"House is empty," Penn announced as he turned towards the kitchen. "I'm going to search for food, medicine, water… anything I can find."

"Do you need any help?" I asked taking a step towards him.

"No, no. Stay here. Rest." He flapped his hand downward. It seemed as though maybe he wanted to be alone, so I didn't press. I'd give him some time before harassing him to get his own rest.

Alice practically fell onto the sofa and Sienna curled up on the loveseat. There was another recliner, but instead I just flopped down on the floor and stretched out my arms and legs.

I breathed in and slowly let the air leave my lungs. My eyelids were already threatening to close, and I didn't think I was going to fight them. I gave in to sleep. I let it wash over me from my toes all the way to the top of my head. It may not have been the smartest or the safest thing to do, but my body had reached its limit.

It was a deep sleep, and I didn't wake up until sometime in the middle of the night. I could hear someone was up and they were very sick.

Chapter twenty-one.

Penn must have found some candles while I'd been asleep because there was a single candle on the dining room table. I wasn't sure if he still had his junky lighter or if he'd found a new one, but the candle was flickering its light on the ceiling and walls. There must have been a second candle too, because there was a glow coming from the bathroom.

I looked around the room and saw Alice was laying on the sofa. Dean's head was cranked to the side while he slept in the recliner and Penn was lying on the floor near the dining room table.

The candlelight waved back and forth in his opened eyes. He stared back at me, but I couldn't figure out what he was thinking, his face was hidden by the darkness.

"You should be resting," I said softly, but shook my head. That hadn't been what I'd wanted to ask. "What's going on in there?"

"It's Sienna... Carter's with her," Penn said making sure his voice was barely audible. He didn't want to wake anyone up. Although, they'd probably wake soon from the noises coming from the bathroom.

Carter started talking to her once she finished dry-heaving. I wondered what had happened to make her throw up. Maybe that's how it started... or maybe Sienna had it worse. Much worse.

"You have to get better... you will get better... for me. I need you," Carter said his voice quiet, but still he said it with such force. He wanted her to believe his words as if that would somehow help her overcome the illness.

I couldn't understand what Sienna was trying to say, at least not at first, but after she cleared her throat and stopped sobbing for a minute, I was able to make it out.

"I love you." She started sobbing again. Sienna sobbed so hard it made her cough, "I don't even care that it's too soon to say that... I just do."

She broke out into another coughing fit followed by more dry-heaves. I saw the jug of water sitting on the table near the candle. There was even less of it now, but I wondered if I should bring it to her. Surely I could find a cup in the kitchen so she wouldn't spread the germs on the whole jug.

"Did you find any more water?" I asked and Penn shook his head side-to-side.

"But I did find a van in the garage. As soon as the sun comes out we are out of here," Penn said softly as he crossed his arms over his chest like he was lying in a coffin. His gun was in his hand.

"Are you sure that's a good idea? She seems pretty sick," I said watching the light dance on the wall near the bathroom.

"There isn't anything here for us, so yeah, I think it's the right thing to do. We have a shelter, but we are almost out of water. At the very least we have to find water."

"Then you better get some rest. Go ahead...
I'm awake now. I'll wake you if something
happens," I said as I sat up and crossed my legs and
rested my chin in my palm. I started drawing
patterns in the carpet with my finger.

He didn't respond. Sleep probably found
him quickly when he gave in to it. Since I'd known
him, out of all of us, he'd gotten the least amount of
sleep. I'm sure it hadn't been good for his body or
his mind, but at the same time I understood it. I
think he felt as though he had to protect us, that he
still wanted to prove he wasn't part of HOME, and
if he went to sleep, he wasn't doing his job.

Carter guided Sienna back into the living
room holding most of her weight. He glanced at
me, but quickly ignored my presence as he turned
his attentions back to Sienna. He helped her back
down on the loveseat.

"Are you OK?" I whispered. Sienna didn't
answer me and instead gently nodded her head.
They had left the candle in the bathroom so I
couldn't help but think there was a possibility
they'd have to rush back.

He laid down next to her and cradled her in
his arm. Carter was letting her use him as a pillow,
and at that moment she looked as comfortable as
possible. He lightly kissed her forehead, and I
looked away when he started gently moving the
strands of hair out of her face.

I wasn't sure how much time had passed,
but I was having trouble staying awake. Even
though I was sitting up, my eyes would close, and

223

I'd startle myself awake.

If Alice hadn't started moaning and whimpering, I wouldn't have been able to keep my eyes open. I couldn't tell if she was awake or not, her body would move a little and then she'd make a noise. It almost seemed as though she was in pain… she sounded as though she was in misery.

"Alice?" I whispered softly, not wanting to wake her if she was asleep. At least I didn't think I did.

"Whhaaa?" she groaned. She tried to finish the word, but it seemed as though she couldn't.

"Do you need some water?" I asked crawling towards the sofa on my hands and knees.

"Yessss," she said stretching out the word. She was having difficulty talking, and I didn't think water was going to be able to help with that.

I bolted up to get her a glass from the kitchen. It was dark but the flickering candlelight provided me enough illumination to find a plastic cup. I poured out a small amount of water from the jug and hopped over Penn to get back to Alice.

By the time I returned, she was still. I hadn't been gone that long, but she had fallen back asleep.

"Alice," I said gently moving her shoulder back and forth. "I have your water."

As I moved her something felt off. Something was different about the way her body moved as I tried to shake her awake.

"Alice?" I whispered, moving her to the side so I could see her eyes. "Alice, wake up!"

I heard someone behind me moving around,

but I didn't bother to look. The room seemed to grow brighter… was it morning?

"Alllliiiiiccceeee," I sang out, but I knew something was wrong. I rolled her even further on to her side, trying to hold her body up so she didn't fall off of the sofa.

I looked into her empty, wide-open eyes. And I knew it. I gripped her shoulders and shook as if that would somehow help.

"Alice!" I cried out as I shook her limp body. "I have your water!"

There was a hand on my shoulder and my whole body jerked away as if I thought it was death coming for me too. Alice's body rolled down onto the floor next to me. Her eyes were on me, but they stared right through.

Her lips were blueish and her skin was so white. Only hours ago she was walking and talking. Now here she was laying on the floor.

Tears fell down my cheeks even though I hadn't known her for long. Penn kneeled down in the middle of the floor ignoring her body. He looked at me as if he was concerned about me.

I had seen far too much death. We all had. But when I noticed Carter staring at his sister's body on the floor, the look on his face almost broke me. It showed that he too had seen his share of death, but this body, this was the body of his sister. This one had to be different.

He let out a heart-wrenching cry and buried his face into his hands. Sienna barely moved, but she wrapped her arms around his middle.

A shiver ran through every inch of my body.

It felt as though I was vibrating from the chill. I sat there rocking back and forth with my hands over my ears. I tried not to look at Alice's body while blocking out Carter's painful cries.

Penn moved over to Carter and put his hand on his shoulder. He bowed his head, "You want me to move her from the room? We could bury her? What do you think she'd want?"

He waited patiently for Carter to respond, "I was surprised she'd fought it for as long as she had. Oh Christ! What should I do? I don't even know what she'd want. We never talked about it."

We had to do something. If we just put her out somewhere the dogs would get her, and I was pretty sure that was the last thing anyone would have wanted for her.

"I guess I think we should bury her," Penn said trying to persuade him. Maybe he had already considered what the dog-beasts would do if they got their paws on her.

"OK," Carter said, gently moving Sienna as he tried to stand up. He took a sharp breath in as his shoulders slumped forward, and I wasn't sure if he was going to be able to get off of the sofa.

"I'll look for a shovel… just wait here. Or in the kitchen," Penn said waving his hand at Dean.

"I don't think I want to do this. Or see this," Carter said looking at me with his sad, red eyes.

I choked back my sob and went to him. It wasn't like I'd be good at providing any comfort, but my body carried me towards him and away from Alice's body.

"You don't have to do anything you don't

want to do," I said leaning against the armrest of the loveseat. My fingers moved against one another nervously. "No one is going to judge you."

"I'll stay here and take care of Sienna. She needs me," he said looking down at her. Sienna rested her head back in his lap and looked up at him. She had a sparkle in her tired eyes that only he could bring out.

He leaned forward and wrapped his arms around her cradling her. Carter tilted his face down and to the side, hiding it from both of us. I looked away.

I went over to the sofa and yanked off the afghan. My eyes started to fill up with tears again as I draped the blanket over Alice's body before I swallowed hard and left the room.

I sat down at the kitchen table and put my head down into my arms. It felt as though the weight on my shoulders was too heavy. I couldn't carry it any longer. This world was becoming too much for me and I hadn't been the one to lose someone. I wasn't cut out for this world.

After a few minutes I was able to calm my breathing, and I stood up. Dean and Penn came back inside from the garage and I put my hand on Penn's arm to stop him. I quietly told them that Carter didn't want to watch and Penn nodded.

"We should take her out of there," Dean suggested.

I followed them into the living room and stood in the way, hoping to block Carter's view of Dean and Penn taking her body out of the living room. They planned to just move it to the kitchen while they went out back to start digging a hole.

When they were outside, I started scrounging around the kitchen for anything that I could eat. Food should have been the last thing on my mind, but sadly it wasn't. Maybe it hadn't been the illness that had taken Alice, maybe it had been the lack of food and water. I felt more desperate for food than ever before.

I found some cans of food and an old, metal can opener. After opening the cans, I stuck a spoon into the goopy thickness and brought two of the cans to the living room and two of them outside.

There were enough cans for everyone but it still wasn't enough food. We wouldn't ever have enough food. I stood outside watching Dean and Penn take turns digging the hole.

I scraped the sides of the can making sure I didn't miss a single molecule of the soup. Even though it was cold, it tasted fine, maybe even good, but then again anything would have tasted good at this point. Maybe even fish.

"We're all going to catch it," I said sniffing back the tears that were threatening to flood out.

"Let's hope not," Penn said as he rested on the shovel.

I sucked in air, "We are all just too weak. There is no way we'll be able to fight it off."

"You sound like you're giving up," Penn said looking at Dean. But he didn't say anything, he just scooped out a big spoonful of his congealed soup and sucked it down before grabbing the shovel from Penn.

After an hour or so Dean pulled himself up

and out of the hole, "I'm done. This is good enough don't you think?"

I looked down into the hole and put my hand on my stomach. The whole thing felt sickening. I wanted to make sure I could keep my soup down.

Penn stepped up to the edge and looked down. He put his hands on his hips and nodded. They both looked sweaty, dirty and tired.

"It'll do," Penn said and looked towards the house. "He's sure?"

"Want me to ask him again?" I said taking a step towards the house. Penn nodded, and I went back inside reluctantly. I didn't want to have to be the one to bring it up, but it was his sister. Maybe he'd changed his mind and wanted to say goodbye.

When I opened the back door, Carter was in the kitchen crouched down by Alice's body. He had his head down on his arm and his other hand place lightly on top of the afghan.

"Are they ready for her?" he asked knowing it was me without even looking.

"Yeah... you want to come out?"

"No."

He put his mouth down close to where her head would have been under the blanket and whispered something only for her, even though she couldn't hear him anymore. Carter stood up, keeping his back towards me as he walked towards the living room.

"Goodbye, Alice."

Chapter twenty-two.

After they'd finished we all sat in the living room. None of us were able, nor wanted, to sit on or even look at the sofa. We'd sat in silence for a long time before anyone spoke.

"So, there's a van in the garage," Penn announced breaking the silence. "I'm going to start packing it up."

I looked at Dean and then at Sienna, "Maybe one more night?"

I thought that maybe another night of sleep would help Sienna. She was sitting up and looked a bit better, maybe the rest was helping. Or maybe it had been the can of food.

"I don't know," Penn said looking at each one of us. He didn't like staying in one place. It was obvious. If we ever made it to Michigan would things change? Would he be able to relax once we made it to our destination or would he want to keep moving? Maybe he wouldn't ever be able to just stop and try to make somewhere our home. What if he wouldn't be able to stop?

"Maybe we should make this place into our home?" I said looking around. It was fairly secluded, we could make it safe and if we could find Lucy's house again, we knew there were supplies there.

"No," Penn said pressing his fist into the

wall. "There's no water here, and what's left of the food won't last long. We don't know anything about this area and we don't have any ammo."

"We don't know Michigan either," I said shrugging.

"But we don't have ammo," Pcnn said jabbing his finger into his palm. "We can find ammo along the way. If we stay here who knows if we can find anything? Where is the nearest gun shop? What if it's been emptied?"

"What if the other gun shops along the way have been emptied?"

"Then we'll try police stations," Penn said as if he couldn't be more sure leaving this place behind was the best move.

Maybe he was right. There were things we'd have to find. Things to stock up on before we could settle in somewhere. There could be a city close to where we were, but it would take time, energy and gas to try to find anything. And if we couldn't find anything quickly we'd be in sad shape.

In Michigan, or maybe somewhere along the way, we could find some place close to water. First and foremost, we needed water. And this place didn't seem to be near water.

"We'll leave when Sienna's ready," Dean said gripping the armrests of the chair he was in so hard his knuckles turned white. Penn's eyes quickly shifted in Dean's direction, but his body softened when he saw the look on Dean's face. I saw it too. He was filled with worry.

"Don't be dumb," Sienna said with a weak

smile on her face. "I'm mostly fine... just really, really tired, but if we have a van, I can rest as we move."

She started coughing softly at first, but it turned more violent. Her hand was over her mouth and it looked as though it might turn into her throwing up in the bathroom again. Carter held her shoulders gently and looked ready to get her to the bathroom if she needed him to. Dean stared at her.

"Seriously, it's just a bad cough," she said in a rough voice that barely sounded like her own. She'd coughed so much it had actually changed her voice. Not to mention her throat was probably sore. She forced a smile, "Let's go!"

"Well, hold on," Penn said smiling back at her, but he had worry in his eyes too. "I'll pack up as much as I can first. Ros, you check the closets for anything we could use. Dean, can you help me in the kitchen?"

The only thing that really mattered for us right now was getting food and water. At least it was all I could think about, but even still, I took towels, a pail and bandages I'd found in the bathroom closet.

Dean and Penn filled the back of the van up with plastic bags as if they'd went shopping. They'd stuffed the bags with the can opener, cans of food, rice, and half-eaten boxes of noodles. They'd also put the mostly empty jug of water, a pot, and a tea kettle in the back. Inside one of the bags I spotted random cups, one of them was a different color than the others.

"Whoever lived here sure liked soup," I said

looking at the plastic bag that only had the soup cans.

"A couple of those are jars of gravy," Dean said flatly.

"Mmm," I said rubbing my belly.

"Dibs on the gravy?" he asked lightly, jabbing me with his elbow. He was trying to tease me, but I would have gladly slurped down the gravy.

I could tell that Dean's mind wasn't fully on packing. If I had to guess, his thoughts were probably mostly on his sister. I knew he was worried she'd suffer the same fate Alice had.

Everyone was quiet, lost in their own thoughts as we climbed inside the van. Penn must have found the keys at some point because he started the van and we drove away, leaving the small home and Alice's grave behind.

Sienna rested on Carter in the backseat of the van. I leaned forward, looking between the two front seats as we drove down the road in search of the highway.

We'd been on the road for a long while before we found a highway. I wasn't completely sure we were going the right way until we found a sign that was still standing to confirm that we were, in fact, heading east.

I hadn't seen him do it, but at some point back at the farm house, Penn must have cut up a piece of hose. He took it out at every abandoned car we came across, but pretty much everything had been drained, probably months and months ago.

The van wouldn't make it to Michigan

unless we found more than a few drops of gas soon.
I wished I would have never suggested Michigan.

Why hadn't I picked somewhere closer? I
barely even remember my reasoning, but now it was
like a finish line. We had to get there before we
could stop moving.

I had thought of the lakes and the distance
from HOME and the resistance. It seemed like it
would be a good place. But it was so far away.
Maybe it was time to come up with a plan B.

* * *

We drove as far as we could until the van
sputtered to a stop. Dean and Penn looked at one
another as if they hoped the other had a brilliant
suggestion. But neither of them knew what to do.

A droplet of water hit the windshield,
followed by another and then another. I looked up
at the sky. There was a gray cloud blanketing it for
as far as I could see. The sprinkles of rain quickly
turned into a full on downpour.

"Guess we'll wait it out," Penn said tapping
the window. It was coming down so hard against
the van I wondered if it was making tiny drop-size
dents.

The van was parked halfway in the ditch so
that we were slightly blocking the road. It didn't
seem likely that another car would be traveling out
this way, so it probably didn't matter. Anyone
around here that was still alive was probably

staying dry, deep inside whatever hideout they had.

We were somewhere in Iowa. I remembered miles ago reading the sign where the people of Iowa welcomed us. Somehow I doubted the words on the sign were still true.

"We're more than halfway there," Dean said looking over his shoulder at Sienna. She smiled at him, but it didn't even seem as though she knew what he'd said.

"We'll need to find another car. It'd be a long way to go on foot," Penn said as he traced a line of water that rushed down the opposite side of his window.

We sat in the car staring out at the rain for what felt like hours and it still wasn't showing any signs of letting up. Without being able to see the sun in the sky, I couldn't even guess at what time of day it was. All I knew was that it was still day time based on the amount of light trying to push through the gray clouds.

After we all had our fill of the cans of soup, there was little to do but sit there and watch the rain fall. Penn slapped his knee sharply, and I jumped at the unexpected sound.

"Jesus, Penn!" I said digging my fingers into my thighs. "I thought that was a gunshot!"

"Sorry… it's just something occurred to me."

"And that is….?"

"Hand me the pot and the jug," Penn said twisting around in his seat so he was looking back at Carter. He slapped his leg again, "I can't believe I didn't think of this sooner!"

Penn looked out the window as if he was nervous it might stop raining any second. Carter reached over the seat and pulled out the jug. He handed it to me before he turned back around to fish out the pot.

Sienna held herself up while she waited for him to finish. Her body seemed to sway ever so slightly. Carter settled back in his seat and pulled her back into his arms.

She didn't look good which had me worrying even more. She'd gotten rest, food and some water, but it didn't seem to be helping. There were dark circles under her eyes and her lips were cracking. I looked up from her and met Carter's eyes.

"Did she eat anything?" I asked softly.

"Some," he said shaking his head, which I took to mean she hadn't had enough.

"I'm right here," she said as if she was annoyed we were talking about her as if she wasn't there.

"Sorry," I said handing Penn the pot. I turned around and leaned forward in case I could help Penn with his water gathering project.

He scooted away from the door and pushed it open. The volume of the rushing rainwater increased drastically. It was almost too loud.

Penn stuck the pot out and collected the rainwater. The pot filled much quicker than I thought it would.

"It's really coming down," he said as he tried to carefully fill the jug on the console with the water he had collected in the pan. He tried not to spill, but water splashed out and ran down both sides of the console.

"Dude," Dean said moving closer to his door.

"Sorry," Penn muttered. He put the jug of rainwater to his lips and gulped down the water before passing it to Dean. "What do you think?"

"It's good," Dean said nodding at Penn. After he took another drink, he smiled and handed me the jug.

The cool water felt soothing in my mouth. I could feel it as it moved down my throat. A smile spread across my face and I was about to share with Carter and Sienna, but when I looked at her, my smile faded.

"Where's her cup?" I asked holding the jug in midair. We should have probably all used our own cups. Maybe one of us was sick and just not showing symptoms.

"It should be in the back. I took several... one is a different color," Penn said nodding towards the back of the van. Carter reached over the back seat and dug around inside the bags.

"Found it," he said spinning around and holding out the plastic cup. I filled it halfway with water, but she probably wouldn't even drink that much.

Carter placed a gentle kiss on her forehead as she moved her head towards the cup. He helped her drink several sips of the refreshing liquid.

Sienna nodded and laid back down on Carter. I reached out to take the cup, but he held up his palm and rested it on his knee. He probably was going to try to get her to drink it all, it would just take time.

I had major reservations about sharing the jug with Carter. After all, he'd been closest to Sienna since she'd gotten sick.

"Is there another cup back there for you?" I asked carefully.

"Yeah, I'll get some later," he said looking down at Sienna. "After she finishes."

"Sure," I said nodding. All he was thinking about right now was getting Sienna well, but he'd have to remember to take care of himself too.

Penn worked at filling up the jug while the rain poured down. He didn't care how much he spilled in the van because we'd be leaving it behind as soon as the rain stopped.

The air outside was cool, and it got even cooler when darkness fell around us. We'd been in the van for hours and hours and it was still raining.

Even with how cool the air was outside, the van would get stuffy. Every so often Penn would open the door for fresh air, but the inside of the van cooled down too quickly. When I started to shiver, he'd close the door.

I hoped his seat hadn't been too soaked from the rain that would drip inside every time he opened the door, but it seemed as though the rain was falling straight down. He didn't complain about being wet, but then again, even if he had been soaked he probably wouldn't have complained.

I laid down on the seat thinking about how maybe HOME was up to something. The rain was still coming down, and I worried that maybe it wouldn't stop. HOME would flood out whatever remained of the world.

I didn't bother telling the others about my fears. There was no reason to tell them when I had no reason to think it was anything more than just rain. Perhaps they wcrc all already thinking it anyway.

Sleep didn't come easily in the van. The seat was uncomfortable… I could feel every spring poking through, jabbing at my overly slim body. The noise from the rain was anything but soothing. It was harsh and unrelenting. The metallic clanging noise it made when it pounded into the van made me think of someone banging a wooden spoon against the bottom of a pot.

The rain might have had nothing to do with the fact that I couldn't sleep. It definitely didn't help that every time I closed my eyelids, I saw Alice's dead eyes staring back at me.

At some point everything must have gotten to be too much, and I fell asleep. When I opened my eyes, it was morning. The rain had slowed to a drizzle and I could finally see out of the rain-sprinkled windows.

The ground around us was saturated. There were pools of standing water scattered all around us. We were surrounded by a thick fog that started at the ground and reached up towards the gray clouds.

"Should we go?" Penn said wiping at the window. I knew he was getting anxious to start moving again, which made me nervous he'd never be able to stay in one place.

239

"Sienna's still sleeping," I said looking over my shoulder. "Carter too."

"Dean was too," Dean grumbled and stretched out his long legs until they pressed against the tilted flooring. "Rain stopped?"

"It's definitely slowed down," I said grabbing the jug of water off of the console. I started chugging it without thinking.

"Take it easy on that," Penn said looking over his shoulder at me. "Not sure how much more I'll be able to collect before it stops."

"Oh right… sorry." I replaced the cap and made sure it was on tight. "Are we going to try to carry everything with us?"

Penn shook his head, "I don't think we can. The lighter we are, the faster we'll move and the less energy we'll exert. We'll take one bag… I'll carry it."

We probably didn't even have that many cans of food left. If we all ate one before we left maybe they'd be gone. The most important thing to take with was the jug of water.

Something pressed against the back of my seat and I turned to see Carter trying to stretch out. He blinked a few times and then looked at Sienna. His movements must have woken her. She tried to sit up but needed Carter to help her because she didn't have the energy. I was beyond worried. What were we going to do for her? What could we do for her? I had no idea how she was going to be able to walk anywhere.

I had hoped that with rest she would get better, but she wasn't. She was getting worse, and it

240

was happening fast. Sienna looked at me and scrunched up her face, annoyed that I was looking at her.

"I'm fine," she said between her clenched teeth. Then she coughed several times before turning to Carter, "Could I get some water?"

He reached down and pulled up her cup. It still had water in it from the last time I had filled it.

"Bring that with," Penn said as he opened his door. "Alright, let's get going."

"Hold on a second. Let's eat anything we aren't going to take with us," I suggested. There was no point in letting anything go to waste if we didn't have to. He nodded once, stepped out of the van, opened the hatch and started sorting through the items.

I couldn't see what he was putting into the bag he was going to take with us. He started passing cans over the back seat to Carter to split up between the five of us.

"One can left… I'll take it with. And the rice, tea kettle, bandages. Think I could make rice in the tea kettle? I'll put it all in the pail," he said with a smile as he lifted up the can opener and dropped it inside with everything else.

Once we were finished eating our cold, overly salty soup, we were off. We walked down the wet, muddy and mucky road. I was about ninety percent sure we were going in the right direction.

We hadn't walked for long before we were at the top of a low hill looking down at what had once been a small town. The whole place was flooded under varying amounts of water.

"Should we try to go around?" I asked looking to see if I could find higher ground. The fog all around us limited my ability to see, but it looked as though we were standing on a peninsula, and the only thing around us was the dirty pool of water.

"It doesn't look too bad," Penn said looking down at our feet. The water levels seemed to be increasing as we stood there and, before long, we'd be standing in the water even if we stayed here.

The cold water started to seep into my shoes making my feet feel numb. My clothes were already damp from walking in the drizzle and fog. I shivered and hugged my body.

I looked out at the city streets trying to see if I could guess at how deep the water was, but it seemed to vary wildly depending on where I looked. It appeared to me as though the city was being sucked up into the earth. I let out a long breath, "If only we had a boat."

Penn took about four steps and the water was already up to his ankles. He turned around, "We can do this. Let's just be sure not to go that way."

He pointed downhill about a block away where the water was almost halfway up the still-standing stop sign post. I sloshed through the water behind him. Carter was helping Sienna along, practically carrying her.

I didn't even think about turning back until we were about four blocks away from where we had stood and the water seemed to be rising up around me. It was like I was standing in a bathtub as it was being filled, and before I knew it, the water was up to my calves. And then up to my knees.

Chapter twenty-three.

The water was pooling up around us so fast I was sure I'd have to start swimming. I didn't know, though, if I had enough energy to actually swim. It was probably just my imagination, but it felt as though the brown, dirty water was thicker than regular, clean water.

Dean grabbed my hand. He looked as though he was afraid of losing me to a current, like what had happened to Sienna back at the river.

"This way," Penn shouted waving his hand to our right, but it didn't matter which way we went. We weren't going to be able to escape the water. It just kept getting deeper and deeper, making it harder to walk.

I looked behind to make sure Carter and Sienna were still with us. Carter was stomping through the water carrying Sienna in his arms. He looked like some kind of superhero that had just finished a battle, whereas she looked like a floppy, rag doll.

"There," Penn said and pointed to an area that seemed to be on higher ground. At least for now anyway. There was a fence with a rusting, broken swing-set surrounded by some trees.

I let go of Dean's hand so I could move faster through the water. It was almost up to my waist and I wanted to be able to use my arms to help me wade through the water. The sooner I could get to that fenced-in area, the better I'd feel.

I took a step to the side, and the earth shifted below my foot. My body fell as if I weighed a ton and, before I could say anything, I was under the water.

It felt as though something was pulling me downward. I tried to swim against it, but it wasn't working. My body felt too heavy and I struggled to break through the surface.

I moved my arms and kicked as hard as I could. My head popped through the water and I gasped for air. Whatever was below was trying to bring me back down again, but I fought against it as hard as I could.

I tried to find Dean or Penn but I must have been turned around the other way because I didn't see anything but water and debris. I tried to shout for them, but no one answered.

"Where—" I started, but I was cut off when I was pulled back under. I hadn't even been able to take in a good breath.

My arms and legs moved frantically and I couldn't get myself up. I started to panic and almost opened my mouth to scream. No matter how hard I swam I couldn't make my body go up. I wasn't even sure I knew which way up was.

Then something happened. A thought occurred to me. Maybe it was just my time. Life above the surface had been hard, and now it would be so easy to just… let go.

My arms were tired and my legs were getting sore. It felt like I was swimming in gallons of thick maple syrup.

"Ros!" I thought I could hear someone calling out for me through the water, but I was probably only imagining it. I was so tired... I just wanted to stop. Dean would keep fighting. And so would Sienna. We'd made a deal. They'd miss me but they'd just have to keep going, same as I would do if I ever lost either one of them.

My eyes were closed but the darkness only seemed to get darker. Maybe I was going deeper, or maybe I was close to death. It felt as though something was pulling at my arm. I must have gotten flipped upside down and whatever it was that used to be pulling at my legs, was now pulling at my arms. Maybe it was time for me to leave my body.

I reached out my hand to whatever it was that was taking me away, to let them know I was ready. It felt like fingers wrapping around my wrist and pulling hard for me to come along. I kicked my legs with my last bit of energy and went with whatever was guiding me away.

When my head broke through the water's surface my mouth opened automatically and oxygen was being pushed into my lungs. It felt like my chest was burning. I looked around blinking rapidly, trying to make sense of what I was seeing.

Penn was in the water holding me up. He grabbed me tightly and swam me over towards the others who were standing near the fenced-in area we'd spotted before.

I started to cry when I saw Dean. Or maybe it was from the pressure I felt in my chest. I was gasping for air and choking on water that must have somehow gotten into my lungs. It felt as though there wasn't enough air in the world to satisfy my need for oxygen.

"Are you OK? Is she OK?" Dean said pulling me closer to him.

I nodded, but my eyes were wide and filled with fear. My body was shaking uncontrollably but somehow I was still alive. At least I was pretty sure I was.

"The ground was under me but then it was gone. Just like that," I said between each breath. "Did I die?"

Dean shook his head, "Still alive. Thank God."

"I think I almost died."

Dean hugged me, "I saw you go under. Looked like something pulled you down. I wasn't sure if anyone would get to you in time. Then we lost sight of you."

"OK," I said not really understanding what any of his words meant.

"Let's get out of here before the whole area is sucked away," Carter said pointing towards a road that went up a hill. "That way!"

Even though I had no energy, I ran for the road holding on to Dean's hand far too tightly. He didn't complain, and I never wanted to let go of him ever again.

I noticed that no one was carrying our pail of supplies, or the jug of water.

"Where's all our stuff?" I said looking at what seemed to be a lake behind me. If we saw them floating maybe we could just swim back for them, but all I saw when I looked back was the brown, mucky water that had tried to swallow me alive.

The water flowed as if it had somewhere to go. I watched the debris moving chaotically around as it was pulled in different directions.

"It's gone," Penn said, and I wondered if he had dropped it so that he could rescue me. I didn't want to be the reason we didn't have any of our supplies. "It's OK. We'll find more."

Once we were at the top of the hill, I knew we were going to be all right. The drizzle had stopped and the only flowing water I could see was the water behind us. The area to the front and sides was saturated from the rains, but at least it wasn't flooded.

I wrapped my arms around my shivering body. Dean put his arm around me, trying to provide warmth, as we walked on the squishy ground.

We were walking through some kind of field, and with each step the earth held onto my foot. My legs were already tired from kicking, but I had to force them to keep going. I didn't have a choice, there wasn't a house in sight.

Even though the rain had stopped, the fog was still relatively thick. There could have been a house in walking distance and we just weren't able to see it.

Sienna started coughing and fell to her knees. Dean ran to her and Carter crouched down putting his hand on her shoulder. He was obviously concerned, but at the same time I knew he had seen this all before with his sister.

"You OK?" Dean said tilting her face up towards his once she stopped coughing.

She stared into his eyes and then her lip started to quiver. "NO!" she cried out. Sienna was done pretending, and I didn't blame her. She was tough, but she was also human, "I'm cold, I'm tired and I'm sick!"

Dean looked at Carter as if he wanted to be told how to make her better, but Carter looked away from him. If he had the answer to that question surely he would have done whatever it was for his sister.

Carter couldn't bear to see the look in Dean's eyes. He recognized the pain, worry and helplessness, as he had once had the same look too.

"We have to find someplace to go," Dean said looking as though he was begging Penn to find something.

Penn nodded, "We will. First place we find we'll stay. No matter what."

And I knew that meant he'd kill if he had to. Penn would do whatever it took to secure the next place we came across.

* * *

When I saw the little house with a small barn off to the side, I was sure it couldn't be real. But when the others noticed it too, I realized it must have been. There wasn't a single one of us that wasn't ready for a break.

Not only did I want to find somewhere for Sienna to rest and get well, I wanted to dry off and maybe find a change of clothes. A shower would be a dream come true, but I knew that wasn't a possibility.

Dean and I didn't even bother holding our unloaded guns as we approached. Carter and Penn checked it out and quickly made sure the house was empty.

I wasn't surprised that houses were empty. It would have been impossible to stay somewhere that didn't have some kind of source for water and food. And even places that did have stocked supplies would run out eventually, unless someone kept working on replenishing them.

Most people probably went out right away looking for help, or others, just like we had when we left the shelter. Those that stayed in their homes probably abandoned them once the food and water were gone.

Eventually those people would find HOME, a different group trying to survive like the resistance, or they would die. There were probably very few people still wandering around like we were. The people that were left in the world were grouped together, hiding or dead. The last being the same fate we'd most likely suffer.

"No one is here," Carter said waving us inside. He helped Sienna to the sofa and Dean followed behind them.

I closed and locked the door once we were

all safely inside. The living room was a mess. I didn't know if it was from the storms that had blown through or if the house had belonged to a family that had just been messy.

There were kids' toys strewn about, dirty dishes still in the sink and what I hoped was fruit juice stains all over the carpet.

"Fireplace," I said looking at it as if I could tell if it would be usable or not.

"Yeah," Penn said sweeping his arms outward, "and fire hazards."

There were three bedrooms and all of them had mountains of laundry stacked and piled in them. It looked as though one of the parents had to stop in the middle of folding the laundry.

I went through the things that had belonged to the mother and found a change of clothing. They didn't fit right... the sweatpants were too baggy, but I was able to tighten the drawstring enough to keep them up. The t-shirt I'd found hung off of me like I was a hanger.

There was a thick coating of dust on the full-length mirror. I picked up a random piece of clothing and wiped it clean. The person staring back at me was almost unrecognizable. My cheeks were sunken in and I was drastically underweight. The girl looking back at me was just a skeleton, and she didn't look happy about it.

It wouldn't even matter if I caught Sienna's cold or not, if we didn't find more food and water soon, it would be too late for all of us.

When I came back out, Penn was digging through the kitchen cabinets. He'd set out several things on the table, but just as with everything else we'd found, it wouldn't be enough. Maybe enough that we could tack on just one more day to whatever our short life expectancy had dwindled down to.

My legs were about to give out, so I went into the living room. I couldn't believe how sore my arms were from having to fight against the waters. I didn't want to know what my burn looked like after the bandage had been soaked in that scummy water.

Dean was sitting on a wobbly chair he'd taken from the dining room. He'd pulled it right up to the sofa so he could be close to Sienna if she needed anything. He was leaning forward resting his elbows on his knees and his forehead down against his fists. I wanted to be there for him, but I didn't know what to do or say that could make him feel better. I put my hand on his shoulder and held it there for a moment before sitting down in a squeaky recliner.

Carter had his back pressed against the sofa. His knees were bent and his feet flat against the floor. He stared at his hands as he passed a tiny red ball back and forth from one hand to the other.

"Can I get her anything?" I asked, even though I had no idea what I could get her. What she really needed was a doctor, and I definitely couldn't get her one of those. All we could really do for her was let her rest, try to find her some food and water, and hope she could quickly fight off the nasty illness.

Dean shook his head. I didn't know if that meant there wasn't anything, or if he didn't know what she needed. Maybe it meant both.

I rocked the noisy recliner back and forth and let my eyes close. Every so often I'd open them and everyone would be in a different position. Everyone except for Sienna.

She was laying on her back with her eyes closed. I couldn't tell if she was sleeping, but I hoped that she was.

I must have fallen asleep because I woke to something warming my body. The heat made my arm tingle, but it warmed my chilled bones. There was a fire glowing and crackling in the fireplace, that I assumed Penn had started.

Sometime after my body warmed I must have fallen asleep again, because I was being woken by someone pushing a bowl of what looked like plain boiled noodles against my stomach.

I squinted at them as if I couldn't tell if I was in a dream, "Noodles? How do we have noodles?"

"There's a big pond out back," Penn said with a quick smile. "Technically I don't think it's supposed to be there, but it is… from all the rain. I boiled the water, then boiled the noodles. I added some salt, pepper, and voila! Pond noodles!"

"You make them sound so delicious," I said taking a careful bite. I worried maybe they'd taste like mud or worms, but they didn't. They tasted like normal plain noodles would.

"Well?"

"Not bad. My compliments to the chef," I said with a grin as I took another bite. I finished the bowl in record time, before Sienna had even taken her first bite.

Dean propped her up and Carter was trying to feed her. She didn't even have the energy to chew the noodles. They just fell out of her mouth and onto her shirt. The noodles stayed there until Dean picked them off.

She turned her head slowly to Dean, and I saw her sunken cheeks and eyes. Her skin was so pale it looked pure white like a sheet of paper. It looked as though she was melting away. When she looked in my direction I wasn't even sure if she was looking at me or through me.

"Deaaaa," she moaned, her mouth unable to form the word. She was deteriorating so fast. Swimming in the dirty water, cold, no sleep, little food and water, it had all taken its toll on her already weak body. I didn't know how she could fight this illness if she wasn't eating or drinking.

"Yes, I'm here," he said grabbing her hand. I could tell by his thick, choked-up voice that he was crying.

"Deeaaan-nah," Sienna said trying to enunciate his name as best as she could. "Deeeeaan-ah om dyyyan."

It took me a few minutes, but when I figured out what she was telling him I couldn't stop the tears. I covered my face with my hands. I didn't know if I could watch or listen to any of it. Alice was one thing, but Sienna... well that was different.

I loved her as if she was my sister. Now she was leaving us. And she knew it.

Chapter twenty-four.

I stood up and went to her side. She turned her head towards me and tried to curl her lips to smile, but it didn't really look like a smile.

"Rosss," she said, and I put my hand on top of hers. Her fingers were so purple. I could see the long breaks between each of her breaths.

I wanted to do something for her, anything to stop this from happening. It was nearly impossible to accept, but there wasn't anything I could do for her.

"Sienna," I said wanting to hide my sadness from her, but I couldn't. I wanted to be strong for her, but I failed. "I love you."

She blinked and the corner of her mouth turned up, she looked happy for just a moment. Her lips moved slowly, "loow oo."

There was so much more I wanted to say, should have said, but I couldn't think of any of it. All I could think about was that this was not how this was supposed to go. This wasn't how I wanted to remember her. I lightly squeezed her hand and left the room.

I went into the kitchen and pressed my back into the wall. My body slid down to the ground as I pressed my palms against my ears as hard as I could.

I didn't want to hear Dean talking to her.

Anything he would tell her would break my heart into so many tiny pieces I'd never be able to put myself together again.

And then Carter too. Although they hadn't known each other for long, I saw how he felt about her almost right from the start. It was nearly instant. Love at first sight... maybe soulmates. Whatever it was, it had been very real.

Just thinking about all the things he'd tell her was almost too much to bear. It wasn't fair to him. It wasn't fair to any of us. And it certainly wasn't fair to her.

After several minutes Penn walked into the kitchen. He didn't say anything he just sat down next to me. I put my head down on his shoulder and I cried until I didn't have any tears left.

I couldn't even guess at how much time had passed when I saw Dean and Carter standing in the entrance way to the kitchen. I saw their red, pain-filled eyes and I knew she was gone.

* * *

Dean and Carter both helped Penn dig a hole for Sienna's body under a large, saggy tree. It was as if even the tree was saddened by what the world had lost.

The ground was so soggy I wasn't even sure if they'd be able to dig a sufficient hole. But once they got started, they didn't stop for a break. They were able to manage a fairly decent sized hole which, thankfully, didn't cave in on itself.

I collected rocks from around the yard while they worked. Maybe I should have stayed in the house to guard it in case someone came wandering around, but I couldn't be in there alone. My thoughts would have gotten the best of me. Picking the rocks kept my mind slightly distracted from it all.

After they finished, Dean, Carter and Penn carried her out. It was unintentional, but it was done very ceremoniously. They all looked straight ahead. Tears streamed down Dean's face and it looked like Penn was biting his lip to stop himself from crying.

They lowered her down wearing faces that looked like they were made out of stone. Dean clenched his teeth as he looked out at the horizon and shoveled in a scoop of the heavy, wet dirt. He passed the shovel to Carter so that he could do the same.

Carter's shoulders were slumped down, but he managed to toss in some dirt before his body started jerking as he let out his cries. He dropped the shovel and fell down to his knees. He reached down to try to stroke her hair.

"No... why? No," he wailed, and Penn quickly got him to his feet. Carter fell backwards and sat in the mud. Penn picked up the shovel and started to throw in dirt.

Dean just stood there like a statue. I wasn't even sure if he was breathing. He looked as though he'd been completely emptied.

I looked away from the hole so I wouldn't

have to watch as Penn covered her with the mud.
My mind wanted to remember her when she was
smiling or laughing.

I would think about how we'd shared a room
in the shelter... that hadn't even felt like the same
life anymore. Or her face when she'd seen me at
HOME after they'd thought I was dead. Her pink-
tinged cheeks and perfect smile when she'd first
met Carter. Those were the things I wanted to
remember. Not this.

When Penn finally finished filling in the
hole, he started packing it down with the back of the
shovel. He was being careful to do it as
respectfully as he could. I walked over to the patch
of dirt and laid out the rocks I'd collected to make a
heart shape. She would have liked it.

I looked down at the heart and bit my lip so
I wouldn't cry. I whispered my goodbye and
followed the boys back inside the house.

Chapter twenty-five.

When we got into the house, the guys took turns changing into whatever they could find. Carter only fit into a pair of pajama pants, but he didn't care. He could have been naked and he probably wouldn't have cared or even realized. What he was wearing was the last thing he would be thinking about.

Penn fell asleep on the living room floor next to the pile of kids' toys. He was exhausted from not only all the digging, but everything else too. His body and mind had hit their limit.

I got him a blanket from one of the bedrooms and covered him. The more sleep Penn got the better it was for all of us.

Dean hadn't said anything since it happened. He'd look up at me from time to time like he wanted to say something but then he'd turn away. All I could do was take his hand and tell him I was there for him.

If I could have, I would have taken away all of his pain, but I didn't know how. He'd just lost his sister. He had every right to feel everything he was feeling.

After we'd lost Owen, he'd disappeared from himself for awhile too, and Sienna would be worse. I would be waiting for him when he came back to me.

Carter was beside himself. He couldn't sit still. One minute he was in a chair rocking himself, the next staring out of the window and seconds after that he'd be pacing up and down the short hallway.

"Can I get you anything?" I asked when he went back to stare out the window. Penn had found and filled several containers with boiled pond water so we would have water if we needed it. "Maybe something to drink, or something to eat?"

"No," he said looking out at the big, saggy tree. He turned towards me, his eyes puffy, "I mean, no thank you."

When night rolled around, Carter would try to lay down but after five minutes he'd be up moving around or staring out the back window again. Penn was still asleep, and I didn't bother to wake him. I'd sleep later.

Dean looked as though he was trying to sleep but, understandably, it appeared to be a challenge for him. He couldn't get comfortable. There were a couple times he fell asleep, but he didn't stay asleep for very long.

I rocked the chair back and forth listening to the silence, trying to fill my mind with thoughts of Michigan. Even though I started to feel tired, I stayed awake. Someone needed to keep watch in case something happened or someone came snooping around. Even though it was the middle of the night in the middle of nowhere.

"Why don't you try to get some sleep... I'm up anyway," Carter said, standing over me. He looked down at me with wide eyes and stared at me awkwardly. Carter was a mess. It was obvious he needed rest. He looked as though he was in a daze not even sure where he was.

"You sure?" I said not really believing he was OK to keep watch. I wasn't even sure if I could fall asleep, but I needed rest too, before I was stuck in the same haze that had captured Dean and Carter.

"Yes. I'm sure," he said and started coughing. He covered his mouth with one hand and pressed his palm against the wall to brace himself.

"Oh, no," I whispered.

"I think so… not sure. But I'd been with Alice through it all and never got sick."

Maybe he had been healthier back at the resistance camp. He'd certainly been far less worn out. They fed him and probably for every meal. He likely could get all the rest he wanted whenever he needed it. Being with us was a different story.

"It could just be a cough," I said with a tight-lipped smile. I tried to look positive, but I don't think I was able to pull it off.

"Sure… maybe," he said and went back to stare out the window some more.

I curled up in the chair and rested my head against my bent arm. It was comfortable enough, and as long as I didn't think about what happened, I was pretty sure sleep would find me. I was worn out. The room started to disappear into the darkness of my closed eyes and I must have fallen into a deep sleep.

BANG!

I jerked awake and looked around the room. Some kind of loud noise had startled me, but I wasn't sure if it was just part of my dream or something that had really happened.

Penn must have heard it too because he was moving. He pushed his body up slightly off of the floor and looked around.

"Did you hear something too?" I asked keeping my voice low.

"Yeah... I think so." Penn blinked his eyes a few times. It seemed as though he still wasn't sure if he was awake.

"Where's Dean?" I asked looking at the empty space where he had been when I fell asleep. I didn't hear Carter pacing the hallway, and he wasn't staring out the window either. "And Carter too?"

They were probably in the kitchen finally allowing themselves to have some food and water. Their bodies needs had probably become too much, and they had to give in, even if they didn't want to. Survival instincts had kicked in.

Penn got up and went to the kitchen but crossed back towards the hallway shaking his head. I could tell by the look on his face they weren't in there. Each door in the hallway creaked as Penn pushed them open one by one.

I got up to watch, narrowing my eyes with each door. Then he pressed on the bathroom door, but it didn't budge. He glanced at me and then lightly knocked.

The door opened and Carter stepped out. I could tell he had been crying. His eyes were still red and puffy, "Yeah?"

"Oh... sorry. Just wondering where you and

Dean were," Penn said stepping away to give him space to exit the bathroom.

Carter coughed, "Well you found me."

"So where's Dean then?" I asked as I crossed my arms in front of my body. I suddenly started to worry that HOME or the resistance was here and they'd taken Dean.

Penn pulled out his gun as if he had a similar thought. He walked over to the door that led to the garage and opened it so he could peek inside. It didn't seem likely he'd be in the garage, so I walked over to the window, thinking maybe he had gone out to Sienna's tree.

The sunlight shone through the branches and the light danced playfully on the freshly dug up ground. It looked as though the mud was already starting to dry up.

But Dean wasn't there either.

I caught something moving in the corner of my eye. The door on the small barn was gently swinging back and forth in a seemingly light breeze. What would Dean be doing out in the barn?

Penn came up behind me and instantly noticed what I was looking at. He quickly walked out of the house holding his gun as if ready to shoot. Carter and I followed behind, but I didn't bother taking out my gun.

I watched Penn disappear into the barn and then slowly back out. His hand was over his mouth. He looked as though he'd seen a ghost.

"What's going on?" I said squinting as I glanced up at Carter. My eyes quickly shifted back towards Penn who looked troubled.

"Not sure," Carter said putting his hand on my arm, and then we jogged to get closer to Penn. Carter pushed on my shoulder as if to tell me to stay still as he went to the barn door. He stopped and turned towards me with those wide unblinking eyes I'd seen before.

He raised his palms up and slowly walked towards me. I shook my head side-to-side. My stomach felt as though it was closing in on itself, as if it knew something was wrong. I tried to move my feet, but they were so heavy I couldn't even lift them.

Penn stood there staring at the door until he saw me lift a foot and move closer. He grabbed my arm and pulled me back, "No!"

"What?" I said, my hands shaking uncontrollably. "I don't understand."

"No... oh Christ no," Penn said pulling at me as I grew impossibly strong and fought against him. What had they seen? Why weren't they telling me?

"Tell me what's going on!" I screamed. I didn't care who heard me or even if I summoned every dog-beast in existence. I wanted to know what was happening.

"No, no, no, no. Stop! No!" Penn said trying to move me away from the barn. Carter started coming towards me, but he stopped, turned back and closed the barn door before helping Penn push me back into the house.

I tried to fight them both, but I couldn't. I didn't know why they weren't telling me what was going on.

"Fucking tell me! I deserve to know!" I shouted. My voice squeaked as I hit a strange lump in my throat. Tears of frustration started falling down my cheeks. I knew something wasn't right.

"It's Dean," Penn said unable to keep his emotions in check. What was out there that could throw Penn over the edge like this? He'd seen and done terrible things but right now he couldn't even talk straight.

I turned to Carter, "What about Dean? Tell me!"

Penn fell to his knees next to me and grabbed onto my pants. His fingers climbed up my leg until he found my hand and squeezed it.

"Ros, I'm so, so, so sorry to tell you this, but… he's gone," Carter said looking off to the side the second the words left his mouth. I knew that he had told me something, but the words weren't making sense.

"Gone? But where? He left us?" I shook my head not knowing why he'd leave us at a time like this. But what did him leaving us behind have to do with the barn? "Why would he do that?"

Penn sobbed harder.

Carter ignored my questions and still couldn't look at me, "He had bullets left in his gun."

My mind raced back to the noise that had caused me to wake up. The loud banging noise I'd heard. It was a gunshot.

"Oh," I said turning to go to the living room. I wasn't sure where my body was taking me but I felt like I had little to no control over it. My legs felt wobbly, and the room started to spin. I took a few more steps before I stumbled and fell to the ground. My ears were ringing so loudly I thought they were bleeding. I started to stand back up but I couldn't balance with how fast the room was moving and I fell back down.

I raised my head up, but the room was still moving too fast. A warmth flooded my body, starting at my toes and working its way all the way to my throat. I felt like I was going to faint, but instead I opened my mouth and threw up all over the floor.

When I finished, Carter was there to help me up. He whispered, "I got you."

He guided me to the recliner and disappeared into the bathroom. Even though the room was still spinning, I watched as he put the towels down and cleaned up my mess.

I saw Penn still kneeling on the floor. Carter reached out his hand to him and after a minute or so, Penn sniffed and accepted the help. They both came into the living room. Carter pulled up a chair next to me and Penn sat by my feet with his back against the chair.

We sat together in silence.

Chapter twenty-six.

I didn't know how I got there but I was standing in the middle of the living room. My body was turned, and I was facing the window but I was too far away from it to actually see anything. Sweat was dripping down my forehead and my heart was racing.

My eyes were so hot it felt like they were burning my eyelids. I blinked and rubbed at them, but I couldn't get any tears out to try and soothe them. I didn't have anything left.

"Did you have a nightmare?" Carter asked softly as he placed his hands on my shoulders. He tried to guide me back towards the chair.

"I think so." I looked around as everything seemed to come back into focus. "Maybe not. I don't know?"

I looked at him as if he would be able to tell me, but he just shook his head. It seemed strange to me that after everything he'd lost, he looked as though he was worried about me.

Before I could stop myself, my thoughts were on Dean. I stared in the direction of the barn as if I could see through walls. Carter took my hand into his and sat with me.

I thought about how, when I was drowning in the flood water, that I wanted to just give up. In fact, I did, just seconds before Penn pulled me up to the surface. If he didn't save me, I wouldn't even be sitting here right now. Could I really blame Dean for giving up?

I wouldn't have ever imagined he'd do something like that. It must have been because of the sleep deprivation and lack of food and water, in addition to losing someone incredibly important. He hadn't been thinking straight.

Even though I was mad, sad, frustrated, confused, heartbroken, and feeling very, very alone, I didn't think I was capable of holding it against him. I loved him, but I wished with every ounce of my being he wouldn't have left me behind.

We'd made a promise. Dean, Sienna, and I promised that, no matter what, we'd keep fighting if we lost someone, but he didn't honor that promise. I thought back to when we made it and couldn't even remember if he had actually agreed to it.

It felt selfish to think about, but if he had truly loved me, how had he been able to pull that trigger? Hadn't he even considered what it would do to me?

I had made a promise to Sienna, and I planned on keeping it, no matter how hard it would be. Penn was still with me, but that was different. He hadn't been there with me through everything since day one the same way Dean had.

Now it was just me that remained. I knew my days were numbered, but I would fight until my last breath. Out of all of us, I had been the weak link and now here I was still standing. Still fighting. I couldn't allow myself to give up. Not now.

I'd show them all. And even though they weren't here, it almost felt as though I could hear them cheering for me. Patting me on the back. All of them… Seth, Owen, Ryan, Sienna and Dean. I could see their smiling faces and hear their voices telling me that I could do it. That I would make it.

Tears streamed down my face. I missed them all so very much. I would have to find strength and do it for them. And for myself.

I blinked, and the room came back into focus. Carter was still holding my hand, and I looked down at Penn who was sitting next to me with his head down.

* * *

I lost track of time and somehow it was night. At some point I must have fallen asleep… sleep my body surely needed.

I couldn't even guess at how many days had passed since I'd lost Dean and Sienna. Maybe it had only been a day or two, but really I didn't even bother to pay attention to when the sun rose or set.

Carter or Penn would bring me water or noodles but most of my time was spent in a haze. I looked at Carter's gun laying on the kitchen table. Which brought my mind to Dean's gun that was still out in the barn.

Penn and Carter weren't next to me, but I could hear their voices in the kitchen. They were talking softly, and I tried to make out what they were saying.

They were discussing what to do, if we should bother going to Michigan, or if we should continue traveling looking for help. Carter thought maybe there were others like us out there, but Penn thought we'd just keep moving until eventually HOME found us. They both agreed on one thing, they wanted to do what was best for me, only they couldn't agree on what that was.

I pushed myself out of the chair and wobbled a second. My legs felt strange since I must not have used them in awhile. I silently entered the kitchen and neither of them noticed me. Penn tapped the table with his fingers as if he was studying an invisible map.

They discussed things back and forth, each making their points, as they discussed the pros and cons of going out in search of help. In a way it almost sounded as if they were giving up. That they didn't think we could make our own sanctuary in Michigan.

Penn stood up, his back to me, "We have to do the right thing here… we're running out of time."

"I know… I know… I just don't know," Carter said with a nod.

"Why can't we just go to Michigan as planned?" I said startling them both.

Penn grabbed his chest and spun around almost losing his balance, "Jesus, Ros!"

"Sorry," I said not feeling the least bit sorry. They were in the kitchen discussing our future plans without me. I was far from sorry.

"We can't do this on our own… we tried. We tried hard, but we are losing the fight and losing everyone along the way," Penn said rubbing at his eye. It looked as though he was pressing on the corner so that he wouldn't start to cry.

"Well I'm still going to Michigan. I don't want to get caught up with the resistance or killed by HOME," I crossed my arms and straightened my spine. To me, I still believed we could find our home in Michigan.

Carter shrugged and looked down at his feet, "And how long will we survive in Michigan?"

"What if we can't find anything?" Penn added.

"I don't know. Then we can talk about other plans. We've come this far… I'm not giving up now." I took a deep breath and slowly exhaled, "I'm going with or without you. I hope with, but either way I'm going."

Penn lowered his head and moving it side-to-side ever so slightly, "I don't think you realize that even if we do find a place, we might not be able to find supplies. There is going to be so much work involved. I'm not sure I can do it."

I could see how defeated he felt. He wasn't trying to hide it. Each loss removed a layer of his shell and he was becoming less of a trained ninja and more of a real boy. I mean, normal person.

"I've done it before. Twice actually. Once before we went to Alaska, and once in Alaska, remember that one?" I asked, knowing he did because that's where he found me. "And I did that one all by myself."

"But supplies are gone. It's different now then it was back then. I'm sure you've noticed the difference," Penn said finally meeting my eyes.

I felt determined and angry. If he wanted to give up that was his choice. They could both go off on their own for all I cared. I was doing this.

"OK. Fine," I said trying to keep the anger out of my voice. "You can stay here. I've done it before and I'll do it again. Boil water to drink from the lakes, rivers, streams... whatever I find. I'll catch fish. Grow seeds—"

"But you won't have—"

"It's not going to be easy, but I'm going to do it with or without you," I said, the volume of my voice increasing with every word. "Come if you want to. I hope that you decide to. I'm leaving in the morning."

I stomped out of the room and flopped back down into the squeaky recliner. My hands were shaking, but I was determined. I wasn't sure how far I'd make it on my own with a single bullet in my gun, but I didn't even care. If I died, at least I would die trying.

Their whispers continued after I had left the room, only this time they were quieter. After about ten minutes they came into the living room. Carter grabbed his gun off of the table and looked at me.

"I'm with you," Carter said. His eyes didn't have that same glow they once had, but there was something new in them. Courage? Tenacity? A renewed sense of purpose? It didn't really matter, but it looked as though he had something to prove.

"Of course I am too," Penn said with a puff

of air. He flashed me a half-smile, "It's not like I'd let you go without me."

"Then it's settled. Let's pack up anything we can." I got up and pushed my way between them. I went into the kitchen and started stacking random things on the table. We would fill the car in the garage with everything we could fit inside of it.

Penn and Carter checked to make sure it had gas and that they could get it started, while I went through every cabinet, drawer, and closet I could find. When they came back inside, they informed me that they had found the keys and we had about a half a tank of gas.

I'd found several empty bottles in the recycling bin, which Penn cleaned out in the pond. He rinsed and filled them with water he'd boiled. It wasn't a lot of water but it was far better than no water at all.

Carter and I started packing up the trunk with what I'd gathered so far from the kitchen. We packed half-eaten boxes of noodles, several bags of dried beans that looked like they were twenty years old, and various spices that we'd probably never use. And we still had plenty of room in the trunk for more.

We each picked out random clothes that we hoped would fit and packed them as well. I even took the nearly full bottle of laundry detergent that had been sitting on a shelf in the laundry room. Maybe once we got to our home, I'd be able to wash our clothes. I'd find a way, even if I had to wash them in the lake and dry them on a clothesline. We'd be able to bathe, and we'd have clean clothes.

In the backseat, smashed under the passenger side, was an atlas. It was just like the one I had back when I'd been traveling with my friends to Alaska. Even though that hadn't been a particularly pleasant trip, I hugged the atlas anyway. The old one had been helpful, and maybe with this new one we'd be able to find the best and quickest route to our new home.

"Should I keep watch first?" I asked hugging my knees in the nearly complete darkness. The moon was shining its blue glow in through the window providing us with a little light.

"Don't bother," Penn said stretching out on the floor and tucking his hands behind his head.

"Huh?"

"What's the point? The doors are locked... if someone tries to get inside we'll hear them. I'm not worried about it anymore," Penn said closing his eyes.

I wasn't sure what had caused him to rethink the way we did things. If someone stayed up, maybe we could see a stranger approaching from far enough away that we could escape. I wasn't sure it was a good idea.

I looked to Carter hoping he'd back me up, but he just shrugged, "I think maybe he's right. Sleep is probably more important. Besides, who's going to be wandering around out here?"

It hadn't taken much to convince me. I blamed lack of sleep for the choice Dean had made, maybe Penn did too. And once we found our new home, we'd want to be able to go to sleep without having to wake up every few hours to keep watch. It was too hard on our bodies and minds.

The sooner we went to sleep, the sooner we could wake up and leave for our new home. The one I needed to get to, and part of the reason might have been just to prove that I could do it.

When the sun woke me the next morning, I actually felt better... confident, in control and recharged. As we walked to the car, I made sure I didn't look out the window towards the barn. If this was going to work, I had to focus on the future.

Of course I was going to grieve, but it would have to be in my way. In a way that would allow me to go on living and fighting for my own survival.

"The gun?" I said stopping before I got to the car.

"I got it," Penn said raising up two guns. One of which had been his with a single bullet left and the other that had belonged to Dean with two left. Carter held his gun which probably didn't have many bullets left either, and all I had was my nearly empty gun.

I didn't know when he had gone out to get Dean's gun, but I was glad he had because I wasn't sure I would have been able to.

"You ready?" Penn asked as I sat down in the passenger seat. He had his hands on the keys.

I nodded and he started the car. He shifted the car in reverse and backed us out of the garage. Once we were on the road, he reached over and took my hand as we drove away from the house... away from Sienna... and away from Dean.

As soon as we found a marked road, I opened the atlas and tried to find our location. It didn't take long before I found it on the map and was able to direct Penn the best way to go.

All we had to do was find gas along the way and if we had perfect driving conditions, we could be in Michigan by the end of the day. I smiled as I watched the scenery go by. It had probably been covered with corn fields and grazing cattle once upon a time, but now it was just empty, deserted nothings with random debris scattered about.

It almost felt like I was going home but I didn't know if we would be able to find the place I was imagining in my head. We probably wouldn't, knowing our luck. But for now, I just had to keep the hope alive. It was for my sanity.

We had been lucky and found gas a couple times. We had made good time traveling. There was no sign to indicate the crossing over into another state, maybe there had been one at one time or another, but now there was nothing. I still knew almost the exact minute we had crossed from Indiana into Michigan. It was like I could see our little car traveling along on the atlas and I just knew we were there.

The sun was setting and it would be dark soon. I sighed and couldn't help but smile. I knew I was going to do whatever it took to survive.

***

~ Running Away ~

Books By Kellee L. Greene

Ravaged Land Series
Ravaged Land -Book 1
Finding Home - Book 2
Crashing Down - Book 3
Running Away - Book 4
Book 5 - Coming Fall/Winter 2016

Other Books
The Landing

About the Author

Kellee L. Greene is a stay-at-home-mom to two super awesome and wonderfully sassy children. She loves to read, draw and spend time with her family when she's not writing. Writing and having people read her books has been a long time dream of hers and she's excited to write more. Her favorites genres are Fantasy and Sci-fi. Kellee lives in Wisconsin with her husband, two kids and two cats.

Coming Soon

Kellee is currently working on several new projects, including another series. Please follow Kellee L. Greene on Facebook to be one of the first to hear about what's new.

www.facebook.com/kelleelgreene

Mailing List

Sign up for Kellee L. Greene's newsletter for new releases, sales, cover reveals and more!

http://eepurl.com/bJLmrL

Thank you for reading my novel.

If you liked this story, there are two things you can do to help. The first is to spread the word! Tell family and friends, share it on Facebook, Twitter, Goodreads and similar sites, or buy it as a gift for someone you think might enjoy it.

The second thing you can do to help, is to leave a review.

Reviews are important, especially to new writers, like me, because it's hard to get noticed among all the other great authors. There are so many writers trying to get noticed, and great reviews help new writers stand out from the crowd.

Even if you don't like leaving reviews or don't have time, I'm still extremely happy and excited you read my book. That means the world to me and I thank you from the bottom of my heart.

But if you do have a few minutes, leaving a review will help me build an audience, get noticed, and could make a huge impact on my writing career. It doesn't need to be a long review, a short honest review is just as helpful.

Again, a huge thank you for reading my novel.

~Kellee L. Greene~

Made in the USA
Monee, IL
16 March 2023

30041375R00154